KALPAR

Across Amastica

A Silas & Bundersnoot Novel

First published by Ironhammer Publishing 2024

Copyright © 2024 by Kalpar

All rights reserved. No part of this publication may be reproduced, stored or transmitted in any form or by any means, electronic, mechanical, photocopying, recording, scanning, or otherwise without written permission from the publisher. It is illegal to copy this book, post it to a website, or distribute it by any other means without permission.

Kalpar asserts the moral right to be identified as the author of this work.

First edition

ISBN: 978-1-962547-04-8

Editing by Isabella Betita
Cover art by George Patsouras

This book was professionally typeset on Reedsy.
Find out more at reedsy.com

To Uncle Alex and Aunt Pat, who helped make my first book happen.

Contents

Acknowledgement   ii

I   Across Amastica

Deepwater   3
Eynsworth Castle   20
Elade-voc   51
Losanti   72
Coursuperieur   103
Somewhere Near Tevioch   150

II   Appendix

The Empress Allie   185
The War of Faeborn Succession   188
A Short History of Elade-voc   193
Map of Eastern Amastica   195

About the Author   197
Also by Kalpar   198

Acknowledgement

First I want to thank everyone who contributed to the Kickstarter to publish *Silas & Bundersnoot*, your contributions made it possible for me to make this next book. Special mention goes to my Uncle Alex and Aunt Pat who were extremely excited to help make my books happen. You all are amazing and your funding has allowed me to actually do work as an indie author.

Thanks also goes to all of my readers, everyone who ever said they loved *Silas & Bundersnoot* and were ready for their next adventures. It told me I was at least on to something with my silly little story ideas. You showed up at my book launch party and made me run out of copies, something I didn't expect to do. You waited patiently as I moved and had to put this entire project on hold for over a month. That means a lot.

Thanks goes to the people of Laser's Discord, who continue to be amazing cheerleaders as we all raise each other up. I know some of your names now and some of you have also sent me pictures of your pets. Also thank you to the Council, (you know who you are) the fun we had at the expense of AI grifters helped alleviate my impostor syndrome for at least a little while.

Getting into specific people I have to once again thank Isabella Betita, my editor, who looked at my writing and said "Oh yeah, there's some really good stuff here. But here's what you need to fix." I'm glad that I found an editor who looks forward to reading what I wrote. I also have to thank George Patsouras who was very patient and accommodating as I hired him in the middle of the process and didn't have everything quite ready for the cover art yet but gamely went ahead and made a truly breathtaking view.

As I got to the end of this process there were a couple of people who deserve special credit. First there's Erin Caskey, who beta-read this book and helped find typos that I missed, although we have extreme differences of opinion on where commas go. Extra credit goes to Eazy8 (D.H.) who managed to get a decent-looking map put together based on my scribblings basically at the very last minute in a matter of days.

And of course, thanks always goes to my spouse, Peabody, who wants to know if Bundersnoot has been fed.

I

Across Amastica

Deepwater

"Are we going to eat soon? I'm starving."

"You ate three hours ago." Silas turned the map sideways and frowned in concentration.

"You say those words as if they have meaning." Bundersnoot yawned, revealing his needle sharp teeth. "Feed. Me."

"Bundersnoot, if you're so hungry why don't you go out and hunt up a field mouse or something?" Silas turned the map again trying to make sense of a smudged notation.

"A field mouse?" Bundersnoot sneered. "Ew, they're riddled with parasites and diseases. Last thing I want to do is eat a field mouse. Filthy creatures. Besides, that sounds like work."

Silas pretended to not notice that Waif snuck a piece of dried meat to Bundersnoot, which he immediately consumed. Waif was a small child of indeterminate age who Silas and Bundersnoot had rescued from a cult some time ago. Bundersnoot had proceeded to wrap the poor child around his paw. Silas was going to have to clamp down on that behavior soon or Waif would become utterly corrupted and Bundersnoot would begin to look even rounder than usual.

Silas took a look at the map again and sighed in frustration. "Damn it all to hell and back, I can't make heads or tails of where we should be going." They had been traveling for almost six weeks now to try to find a cure for Silas's condition. Their journey on the imperial highway north from Elade-voc had been swift until they had crossed the Vidange River and left the highway for the meandering back roads which had finally brought them to this particular point. The signposts at the crossroads were no use, the paint so faded by the sun they were completely illegible. "Deepwater should be around here *somewhere*."

"I'm not surprised," Waif said. "How old is that map anyway?"

"It was perfectly fine the last time we came through here."

"How long ago was that? Before the Empire?"

"You hush," Silas sniffed. "It was a mere thirty years ago, if you must know."

"Ah right, after dirt was invented," Waif said.

"Less arguing, more feeding," Bundersnoot added his opinion.

"Bundersnoot, if we fed you as often as you claimed you were hungry you would be a perfect sphere with a diameter of approximately one yard."

"I fail to see a problem with that arrangement." Bundersnoot stretched and jumped down from the wagon. "Well if you're not going to feed me I see little point in staying here." Confidently, he trotted off into the weeds lining the road.

"Should we go after him?" Waif asked.

"No. Bundersnoot can handle himself; anything that he can't outfight he can outrun. Well, almost anything. There was that one incident."

Waif cast a long, worried look at where the cat had seemingly disappeared. "I was more worried about him never coming back, Master Silas."

"He'll come back when he's hungry enough." Silas gave up

on the map and started digging through one of his bags. "I know I packed it when we left Elade-voc. Where on earth did I put... Ah, here we go!" Silas pulled out a carved hickory box kept closed with brass latches. Inside the box was a small device, a flat rectangle about the size of his hand, carefully ensconced in a velvet tray. He carefully removed the device, tapped it twice, and spoke a phrase of Old Amastican to the rectangle. There was a soft chime and the rectangle spoke back to him with a pleasant, professional woman's voice.

"No! I need help finding Deepwater you damned device!" Silas groaned and tried speaking to the device again.

"What on earth is that?" Waif asked.

"This? This is a pocket wizard's tower, a device which is worth a small duchy. Well, maybe a large duchy depending on the quality of the duchy. I found it in my adventuring days when my comrades and I managed to defeat a lich. Goodness, was that really fifteen years ago?"

"But what does it do?"

"It allows me to do a great many things which would normally only be capable with a well-supplied wizard's tower. By expending magical energy, I can read the information in any of the books in my library, as well as any information other practitioners have decided to share with others. With the right permissions I can even access libraries in places as far off as Old Tevioch. In addition, it can calculate the phases of the moon, locations of constellations and planets, and send messages to other people with such devices. Although right now, I am attempting to figure out where we are."

The dubious look on Waif's face had been replaced with more appropriate awe. "That's incredible! Why don't you use it more often?"

"Because it's worth the price of a small duchy," Silas answered promptly. "There are legends that in the very early days of the Amastican Empire, when the Empress still walked the earth, all manner of magical devices were available for even common people. Sadly, with the decline of the empire, much of that knowledge on making devices has been lost and they've become increasingly rare. And finally, if you're unable to connect with other practitioners it's almost useless. For example, I need to get in contact with at least three known locations to determine where on earth we are."

"Known locations?"

"So, a very long time ago, the Amastican Empire tried to figure out exactly how much land they controlled. Starting from the Imperial Palace as point zero, they carefully measured the distance from the palace to other locations like the Imperial Library, the Temple of the Empress's Ascension, so on and so forth. Once they had enough data, with math they could calculate the location of anything within the city of Tevioch. I understand quite a lot of math goes into the process. It took over a hundred years but eventually they were able to chart the entire empire. So if I can get my tower to connect with three known locations, all of which know their positions relative to each other, it can tell us where we are."

There was a chime and the device said something in a language that Waif didn't understand. Silas had, at best, a rudimentary understanding. "Right, we want to turn right at the crossroads and we should reach Deepwater sooner or later. From there it's a few miles to the north road." Silas carefully returned the device to its carrying case and packed the case back in its satchel.

Just as he was about to get the wagon moving again,

they heard Bundersnoot shouting at the top of his lungs. "Silaaaaasss!" Bundersnoot was running up the road as fast as his feet could carry him. "Silaaaaasss! We've got trouble! Serious trouble!" Bundersnoot barely paused before he leapt into the wagon, startling the horse. "We need to turn around, right now!"

"Bundersnoot, what in the name of the Empress has gotten into you?" Silas was trying to calm their horse which had been badly spooked by Bundersnoot's arrival. "Easy, girl! Easy!"

"What's wrong?" Waif asked.

"I smelled cooked chicken so I went off in that direction." Bundersnoot nodded to the right. "And I found a village, but something big and mean stomped that village flat. I could sense magic all over the place. I don't know what wiped out that village but we need to turn this wagon around and find another way around."

"What do you mean stomped flat? What did you see? Any distinguishing marks? And what about the cooked chicken?"

Bundersnoot gave a yowl of dismay. "Silaaaaas, believe me when I say this: we *cannot* fight this. Not without tools, not without preparation."

"What did you *see*?" Silas persisted.

Bundersnoot turned around multiple times to calm himself and then sat down. "There weren't any scorch marks so it wasn't a dragon. Literally every house in the village was destroyed, no two stones left standing. Trolls do not have the patience for that sort of thing. I don't know if this village angered a local warlord or maybe a wizard…"

"Did you find any survivors?" Silas asked.

"No. Silas, everyone in that village is dead."

"Are you sure about that?"

7

"Well, no. I didn't exactly stick around to find out."

"Master Silas, sir, if whatever stomped that village is big as Bundersnoot says it is, shouldn't we put as much distance between us and whatever it was?"

"Yes! The child! Listen to the child!"

Silas managed to turn the horse around and got the wagon pointed towards Deepwater. "If anybody's left alive, we owe it to them to help. If there are no survivors, I'd rather not leave something big and dangerous behind us without knowing what it is. Hyah!" Silas slapped the reins and the horse started cantering towards the village.

Bundersnoot groaned. "Sometimes there's just no reasoning with him."

* * *

Silas stood up and brushed dirt off his robe. "Well it was definitely big, whatever it was. Let's see what else we can induce from the evidence."

They were standing in a field of barley, which had been trampled and burned, the crop entirely ruined. Silas took his staff from Waif and pointed at the hole he'd been examining. "I'm assuming this is a footprint and it's more or less a perfect trapezoid without any toes. Definitely not a natural creature, unless there's a natural creature with perfect trapezoidal legs I haven't heard about. Even most artificial creatures like golems utilize toes so that eliminates a lot of possibilities. As for size, Bundersnoot, how deep would you say this is?"

Bundersnoot jumped down into the hole and promptly curled into a ball, retracting his head. "I'd say a good eight inches deep, Silas."

"The soil here is fairly compactable so evidence points towards something very large and very heavy, although the pattern of these footprints doesn't make a lot of sense."

"Quadruped," Bundersnoot said confidently.

"It doesn't *look* like a quadruped, the spacing is all off."

"For an terrestrial quadruped, yes, but look, think about a crab."

"Crabs have ten legs, Bundersnoot."

"Just look! Assume a circular body, no oval body. Let's call it twenty-five...thirty feet across. Four legs, arranged on either side of both vertexes."

"Should I understand any of that, Master Silas?" Waif asked. "Because it didn't make any sense to me."

"Here, Waif, let me explain." Silas stepped over to a clear patch of dirt and drew an oval with his staff. "Okay you see these points where it looks like somebody took a circle and stretched it out? Each of those is a vertex. So Bundersnoot is saying its body is maybe thirty feet across at the long part and it's got legs....here and here?" Silas made small exes and Bundersnoot nodded at the diagram.

"That would be my guess. And there aren't many artifices that match that description."

Silas chewed his lip in thought. The road to Deepwater was well-traveled and the days of summer were already shortening. There *should* be people out in the fields trying to get the barley crop in as soon as possible. There should even be the hum of insects and the songs of birds on a fine day like this, but everything was eerily quiet. When animals themselves ran away or hid, seasoned adventurers like Silas *knew* something was seriously wrong.

As a group, they walked back to the road and started towards the remains of Deepwater village. Silas had hidden the horse and wagon a mile outside the village in a copse of trees and they had proceeded on foot. "An artifice as big as a house on four legs capable of leveling a village. I don't know many things that fit that description."

"You know exactly *one* thing that fits that description," Bundersnoot said.

"I know, I just don't like thinking about a war construct running loose. Usually the best counter to a war construct is another war construct."

"What's a war construct?" Waif butted in, clearly lost.

"It's a massive machine powered by magic, capable of breaking armies and toppling castles," Silas explained. Silas had seen a battle between war constructs back during the Faeborn War, but what the armored titans did to each other paled in comparison to what they did to human soldiers. He had seen dozens of men vaporized in an intense beam of concentrated magical power, reduced to a handful of ash. They had been the lucky ones compared to the people the construct had trampled.

Silas took a deep breath and tried to clear his mind, lest fear turn to panic and he start making foolish mistakes. "It takes an immense amount of bronze and an entire team of enchanters to get one functional so they're valuable enough that even a broken or malfunctioning construct is worth the effort of retrieving. I don't know how a rogue one ended up in Deepwater of all places."

"Could it be something left over from the civil war?" Bundersnoot asked. "Branch of the Silverbarks got kicked out of the Empire by the Cascades?"

"No, the war ended two decades ago." Silas shook his head. "The last of the Silverbarks escaped across the sea and took every war construct they could get their hands on with them. We would have heard if they'd returned from Oltramar."

"What war was this?" Waif asked. "And who are the Silverbarks and the Cascades?"

"Well, about thirty, thirty-five years ago, Empress-Regent Grâce IX, last of the House of Faeborn, died without a female heir and the mages of the empire had to decide who would inherit the throne. The Silverbark family were more directly related to the Faeborn line and their scion, Rachelle, was the most powerful wizard among the nobility. However, their main power base was here, in the outlying provinces beyond the Braelor Mountains."

"Rachelle's main rival, Lier Cascade, had a power base closer to Tevioch and greater influence with the ruling magocracy. Ultimately the mages decided to hand the throne to Lier, which led to Silverbarks declaring war on the usurpers. The war was long and bitter, but eventually the Cascade branch won and the last of the Silverbarks and their supporters fled across the sea to New Amastica. But the Cascades had expended so much of their strength that they withdrew from most of the lands beyond the Braelors and took their devices with them to secure their rule in the imperial heartlands. It's how Elade-voc became a free city, just sort of slid out of imperial control."

"The Cascades could be trying to re-exert their influence beyond the Braelors," Bundersnoot said, but even he didn't sound convinced by that argument. Deepwater hadn't been a large village, with no more than thirty families in residence. Including animal pens and outbuildings, the village couldn't have held more than a hundred human souls in total. Hardly a strategic asset worth reclaiming.

The party walked into the village and examined the devastation that had been wrought. Every building was rather literally trampled flat, the deep footprints of the—potential—war construct everywhere within the tiny village. Stout timbers, thicker than a grown man, lay snapped and shattered as easily as Waif might bend a dry twig. What little brick and stone had been used in Deepwater's construction were now colored streaks of powder through the dirt lanes of the village.

Silas and Bundersnoot started searching the village for survivors. Silas conjured a circle of blue light between his hands and held it like a servant might hold a platter. A red dot appeared on the edge of the circle towards Silas's left. Silas turned until the dot was straight ahead of him and walked forwards a few paces. The red dot advanced from the edge of the circle and moved towards its center. "This way." Silas said, letting the spell fade into nothingness. "Someone's still alive in this direction.

Bundersnoot navigated the broken houses with ease, jumping over hazards as Silas and Waif struggled to keep up. He perched atop a pile of rubble and beneath it they found a middle-aged woman clinging to life. She looked about forty years old, probably taking over as matriarch of one of Deepwater's farming families as her mother spoiled her grandchildren. Silas knelt down and blue light emanated from his hands as he passed them over the woman.

"I'm sorry," Silas said as he took the woman's hand. "Your injuries are too severe for even my magic to heal. I can try to ease the pain, though."

"I expected as much when I couldn't feel my legs," the woman rasped.

Silas did a small chant and the blue light flowed into the woman. "My name's Silas, and these are Bundersnoot and

Waif. Bundersnoot's the cat."

The woman nodded in greeting. "Helene. Did anybody make it out of the village?"

"I don't know yet," Silas admitted. "Do you know what happened? What attacked your village?"

"It was this great big metal…thing," Helene said, every word hardly more than a whisper. "Big as a house and with massive claws." Silas's heart sank at the description, there was no doubt now that it was anything but a war construct. "A few of the men found something in a cave about a mile from here. They were poking around to see if there was anything useful and they stumbled on it. Our elders told them to leave well enough alone, but I guess they didn't listen. They came running back today and that thing followed them. I was trying to organize people when my house fell on me. That's all I remember."

"That's all right," Silas said. "We'll try to find the others." Helene closed her eyes and Silas let the magic ease her into her final sleep. Then he stood up and re-conjured the circle of light. He slowly rotated so no part of Deepwater was unscanned, but no further red dots appeared. "I'm not seeing anyone else nearby. If anybody's alive they skedaddled long ago. We need to find the local liege lady and let her know a war construct is on the loose."

Suddenly, the ground shook and a steady, repetitive rhythm of thuds grew slowly louder. "Silas, I don't think we're going to have the luxury of running away," Bundersnoot said. "We need to find somewhere to hide." Bundersnoot jumped onto a mess of timbers and scanned the area. "I see the entrance to a cellar right over there." Bundersnoot leapt in the direction of shelter, slipping through a hole between two beams and into the cool cellar below, soon followed by Silas and Waif.

Dusty light filtered in through cracks in the floor above and several holes where the roof of the cellar met the surface level above. Silas climbed onto a barrel and looked through a small hole in the direction of the thudding noise. At first the only sign of the construct's passage was the flight of birds, scattered by its advance, but soon the tarnished bronze body of the construct, coated in a green patina, came into view as it stomped into Deepwater. It stood a good fifty feet tall on its four massive limbs, double jointed and creaking with each ponderous step. The construct also had two arms that ended in massive scythes, still spattered with blood from its recent victims.

The construct drew closer towards their hiding place and dirt trickled down from the cellar's walls. Soon it was directly overhead and Silas could feel the magic of the construct making his teeth itch; he prayed that the earth wouldn't collapse under its weight. The body of the construct blocked the light from above. Silas counted down the seconds, waiting for the construct to continue its search, but it stubbornly remained standing above their hiding place, metal joints creaking as it searched back and forth.

"I think it's trying to find you," Bundersnoot said, crouching low to the ground and eyeing the floor above suspiciously. "It probably hones in on sources of magic."

"So do we wait for it to get bored and go away?" Waif asked.

"Probably the safest plan," Silas said. "Better than trying to…"

Silas's sentence was cut off by a loud thrum and sickly-green light pierced into the cellar. Everyone screamed in surprise, and were further shocked to realize that they were still, at least for the next minute or so, alive.

"What was that?" Waif asked.

"That was a tremendous discharge of magical energy," Silas explained. "Now we wait and see what model of war construct this is." The artifice above them had stopped moving, its joints locked into place to keep it from toppling over, and emitted a high-pitched whine that meant its magical energy was being recharged. Silas slowly counted in his head to sixty and when the walker remained frozen, he let out a breath he didn't realize he'd been holding. "Okay, good, it's not a Mark V. That means we have some time."

"How much time, exactly?" Bundersnoot asked.

"Well, either it's a Mark IV or a Mark III. Ideally, it's a Mark III, which means we have another four minutes before its replenishment is complete and it can walk again."

"Let's pretend I am not an optimistic cat and say it's a Mark IV."

"Well, in that case, we've got less than two minutes left. Fortunately, I have a plan. Possibly."

"Great, what is it?"

"Bundersnoot." Silas hesitated, knowing that this plan was not going to meet Bundersnoot's approval and he really had no time to persuade the cat. "I need you to distract it…"

"I have not grown tired of life and I already hate this plan. Make another one." Bundersnoot began washing his paws when Silas pulled out a little pouch of herbs and began waving it in front of Bundersnoot's face. Bundersnoot's pupils dilated and began following the pouch back and forth with his head. "Ooooooohhh, is that catnip? I wouldn't mind a little…" Bundersnoot stopped and shook his head. "Silas, you stop that right now. I'm not going to fall for your petty tricks, you…"

Bundersnoot's train of thought trailed off when Silas crushed the pouch and pressed it almost against Bundersnoot's nose.

With no further warning, Silas threw the pouch out the cellar and into the daylight above. Bundersnoot darted after it.

"Hahaha, I've got your pouch now, Silas!" Bundersnoot laughed and began rolling in the ground with the catnip. "You've no way of coercing me now, you third-rate... Wait, what was that?" Both Silas and Waif looked up from in the cellar and heard the construct begin walking again in Bundersnoot's direction. A screech, and a loud "I hate you, Silaaaaaaas!" was all they heard as Bundersnoot fled towards the edge of town.

"All right, Waif, I need you to stay here."

"But I want to help."

"And you can help by staying here." Silas hadn't meant to drag a child into mortal peril, but there was nothing he could do about that now. "If Bundersnoot or I don't come back wait until dark. The construct doesn't do so well at night, you should be able to slip back to where we stashed the wagon. You run in any direction and tell them a Mark IV has destroyed Deepwater. Say that back to me."

"A Mark IV has destroyed Deepwater."

"Good, anybody who can do something about it will know what it means."

"But what about Bundersnoot?" Waif looked up towards where the cat was currently running for his life. "Shouldn't we help him?"

"Bundersnoot, despite his complaints, is perfectly capable of taking care of himself. And hopefully so am I."

That said, Silas scrambled up out of the cellar and stopped only briefly to get his bearings and find where the war construct currently was. He sprinted as fast as he could towards the large pool of freshwater at the village's edge, which

16

had given Deepwater its name.

At some point in the distant past, an accident of geology had created a large sinkhole which provided easy access to water and enabled a small farming community to grow up around it. Silas didn't know offhand how deep the natural cistern went, but he was pretty sure it was deep enough to sink the construct. Silas was about a hundred yards from the edge of the sinkhole when he sensed the walker moving towards him. He didn't think he could run any faster than he already was, but somehow, Silas managed to exert even greater speed from his burning limbs and splashed into the pond's shallows.

Silas heard the walker's thuds come to an abrupt stop and he dove beneath the three feet of water. Even under the protection of the water, he was almost blinded by the beam of magical energy. Just when Silas thought his lungs would burst, the walker's attack ended and Silas was able to resurface. "All right, you mechanical menace, let's see how well you can swim." Silas pulled out a lump of quartz from his belt pouch and clasped it in his fist as he murmured words of power. When he opened his fist, the piece of quartz was emitting bright red light, rising a few inches into the air above his hand.

"Let's see how you like chasing phantoms." With a mental push, Silas sent the stone flying across the sinkhole while he remained crouched as far as he could in the water. After a few minutes, the walker whirred back to life. Silas held his breath and waited, hoping that the walker's sensors would be deceived by the illusion he had put on the quartz crystal, instead of just trampling him to death.

The walker slowly marched into the pond, the mud squelching beneath its legs. It tried to lock onto the crystal and eliminate its target with a burst of magic, but Silas kept the crystal weaving erratically and frustrated the construct's efforts. Finally, it charged towards the phantom enemy, scythe arms swinging in an effort to take it out in melee. Too late the walker noticed that it had stepped out with nothing to support it, its forelegs now flailing in open water. There was a groan of machinery as the construct attempted to backtrack onto higher ground but one of its joints snapped under the unaccustomed load and the leg fell limp.

The remaining functional leg slipped in the mud, and its center of gravity tipped over the edge. It would have been more dramatic—with a large splash and a large wave of water—but the construct merely slipped below the surface and disappeared, never to be seen again. Silas remained where he was, counting to sixty. When nothing continued to happen he stood up and began pulling his quartz crystal back towards him. When the quartz crystal passed over the center of the sinkhole, Silas kept it floating in the air for another minute, just to make sure the construct was truly finished. Satisfied, Silas flicked his wrist and the crystal returned to his hand.

Silas squished his way back to dry land and found Bundersnoot waiting for him, perched on a piece of rubble. "Is it gone?" Bundersnoot asked.

"Well, I tricked it into the sinkhole. I'm fairly certain it's trapped down there, but we should still tell the local liege lady so she can make sure of it. There's no guarantee it can't climb back out given enough time." Someone responsible should have taken care of that war construct years ago. Instead the people of Deepwater had paid the price of their carelessness. It was heart-breakingly tragic and Silas felt far wearier than he should. Dealing with pining youths seeking love potions looked downright congenial by comparison.

"I don't recall you ever using that particular trick to disable a walker when you were in the war." Bundersnoot said, pulling Silas back out of his reverie.

"I was only in the war for a couple of weeks, the opportunity never came up. The one battle I was in, the walkers just blasted each other with magic and when that failed charged each other." Silas shuddered at the memory, remembering what had happened to the poor people caught in the middle of that struggle. Silas hadn't really cared who sat on the throne in Tevioch, but pressure from his teacher and friends had made him throw his lot in with the Silverbarks. One battle had been enough to convince him he wasn't cut out for the military life and he quietly un-enlisted shortly afterwards.

Silas wrung out the hem of his robe, managing to get most of the water out. "Well, no sense hanging around here, let's go find Waif."

Eynsworth Castle

"Storm's coming up, I can smell it in the air." Bundersnoot was scanning what sky was visible above the dense old-growth forest. Slate gray clouds hung thick and heavy in the air. "We better get under cover in the next...three hours. Preferably sooner."

"You can tell he's worried. He's stopped demanding food," Silas said and winked at Waif.

"I make perfectly reasonable demands, and are they met? No, I get nothing but abuse! I don't have to stay here and take this, you know!" Bundersnoot sniffed haughtily. "I'm sure Waif and I could have an excellent career chasing mice out of towns. Waif, do you know how to play the flute?"

"Not really," Waif answered.

"All right, you, you've made your point." Silas reached over and gave Bundersnoot an affectionate scratch of the ears. "We should reach Tallpines in an hour or so. I was hoping to arrive at Brynjar's castle tonight but we won't be that lucky."

Jarl Brynjar was a frost giant whose grandfather had erected a mead hall on the mountainside over a thousand years ago. Brynjar's family had ruled over this patch of land either as tributaries of the Empire or in their own right ever since. What was of most interest to Silas was Brynjar's library, a collection of rare texts carefully curated through the centuries. Giants, much like dragons, valued treasure but were unafraid to branch out beyond the usual "pile of shiny metals and gems."

If Brynjar's library didn't have the answers he needed, then Silas had no idea where he should search next. It could have been the change in the weather but the wound from the vampire was bothering him more frequently and he was worried he was running out of time. *Let's hope the Empress is merciful and we find what we need.*

Tallpines started life as a lumber camp that provided raw materials to meet the growing demand for ships' masts. As the demands of oversea trade grew, so did Tallpines. Most of the population were still seasonal workers who came up from the low country to earn a little hard currency during the winter, but a core of permanent residents remained year-round. The center of the village was the massive cookhouse and bunkhouse, where most of the seasonal workers stayed. Arriving at the beginning of autumn meant there were still a few extra bunks for Silas and Waif to use. For a small fee, of course.

"Don't get many travelers this time of year," the landlady said, looking Silas over suspiciously. "Especially not a grown man with a child and a cat. What brings you back our way, stranger?"

"Heading up to Eynsworth Castle. Jarl Brynjar's an old friend of mine and I wanted to poke through his library." Silas saw no reason to obfuscate his purpose. Wizards were perpetually heading towards libraries to dig around in search of one thing or another. The general population usually viewed this behavior with benign confusion.The key word, of course, was "usually."

"Well now, think it's been a good six or seven years since I've heard anything from the Jarl. Can't say I've heard of him having many friends either. I tell you right now, we don't look kindly on people causing trouble round these parts."

Villagers who had experience with adventurers took a dim view of armed vagabonds even at the best of times. Since the war things had become far less certain on this side of the Braelors. "Just stopping to get out of the storm for the night, ma'am. Come morning we'll be on our way."

The landlady didn't seem terribly satisfied with Silas's answer but his silver spoke loudly enough for her to ignore her concerns. Tallpines cuisine tended towards both plentiful and filling, which Waif and Bundersnoot took great pleasure in. Bundersnoot was in the middle of demolishing a ham almost as large as himself and Waif was tucking into their third stack of griddlecakes when Silas finally sat down at the table. "Bundersnoot, I need you to go sit next to that table with the men huddled together." Silas casually pointed in the general direction of a table occupied by five men trying to not look furtive and failing tremendously.

"Every time I finally get a decent meal somebody decides to spoil it," Bundersnoot groused as he picked up the ham and carried it under a table near the obvious schemers.

"Trouble?" Waif asked.

"Definitely trouble, not sure if it's ours yet. But forewarned is forearmed." Silas placed a talisman carved from tiger's eye stone on the table and drew a circle around it with his finger. "Bundersnoot, I call upon thee. Grant me thine ears that I might hear." Suddenly the conversation of the table was audible from the talisman.

"...a professional for sure. If we let him take care of the giant, we could loot the entire castle. There's got to be enough to set all of us for life up there."

"Why wait? We could head up to Eynsworth tonight and take all the choice bits for ourselves."

"A great plan if you hadn't forgotten two things: First of all, it's pissing down rain. And second of all, there's still a giant very much alive up in Eynsworth. You want to go climbing a mountain in the wet and the dark just to get your bones ground into bread?"

"I thought that was just a story they told kids to quit misbehaving."

"Story or no, I'm not risking my neck on a night like this. We can wait until daylight and see if our stranger is really heading up to Eynsworth or not. Then we can decide if we want to follow."

Silas waited a little longer but the conversation drifted to village gossip which he had no desire to listen to. He cut through the circle again with his finger and the talisman became silent. After a sufficiently unsuspicious amount of time passed, Bundersnoot returned to their table. "We're going to need a plan or there will be all manner of trouble," he said, forming a loaf on the table.

"Waif, how good are you at acting unnervingly creepy?" Silas asked.

Waif swallowed their current mouthful of griddlecake and their face went completely blank. "The bone man is coming, soon you'll all be dead. The bone man is coming, to bash your lying head. The bone man is coming, for your sins you'll pay. The bone man is coming, it's too late to pray," they said in a strange, childish sing-song. Both Silas and Bundersnoot stared at them with utter shock. "Was that good enough?" Waif asked, returning to their normal voice.

"Waif, where the hell did you learn a song like that?" Silas asked.

"Oh, we kids in the slums loved trying to scare each other with that one all the time. Was it creepy enough?"

"Waif, with a little prestidigitation, I think we could scare an entire army with that song."

* * *

"They're coming up the road now," Bundersnoot said from his perch on an elm tree above them. "We've got maybe five minutes."

Silas looked Waif over. He was no expert in cosmetics but he had learned a thing or two from Robèrta back in the day and was able to at least make Waif look unnaturally pale and hollow-eyed. "You have your lines ready?" Silas asked.

"I think so. Sing the bone man song and then just act creepy?"

"That's the gist of it. Remember, everything you see is going to be an illusion, the only dangerous things are going to be the men from the village. Nothing else that you see will be able to hurt you."

"I know." Waif smiled and then headed towards the road, skipping like children the world over. Silas took a look over his illusions again to make sure there were no obvious giveaways. He had to admit, he may have overdone it with the hanged men in the trees but he was particularly proud of the skulls bleeding out of their eye sockets. Silas crouched down behind a fallen tree that served as an improvised hunting blind and watched.

There were about ten men from the village, more than had

EYNSWORTH CASTLE

been at the table last night but not so many as to make Silas worried. Right now they were occupied primarily with the mud created by last night's rain rather than anything on the trail ahead of them. They only looked up when, out of sight, Waif started singing loudly and enthusiastically; with a simple spell Silas was able to redirect Waif's voice so the villagers were unable to determine exactly where they were hiding. All of the villagers immediately paled at the grisly illusions that Silas had conjured and a few looked ready to beat a hasty retreat.

"We've worked in these woods our entire lives, there's nothing to be afraid of here!" the man, who Silas assumed was the ringleader, tried to stiffen his followers' resolve. "Somebody's trying to scare us off! Probably that wizard that came through last night. Are we going to let some outsider loot everything of value in Eynsworth?" The followers mumbled something like agreement and the group was ready to start up the road again when Waif started singing again.

This time Waif emerged from their hiding place and started skipping towards the men. One of the men in the back of the group immediately decided he had had enough and discreetly ran back towards Tallpines, leaving his comrades to deal with whatever fresh hell this represented. Their song completed, Waif came to a stop and giggled. "Whatcha doing out here, misters?" they asked, tilting their head to one side. "You coming to meet the bone man?"

"What the hell are you talking about, child?" the ringleader asked. "Where are your parents?"

"Oh, they're gone now. Gone to meet the bone man." Silas made the bleeding skulls rattle and laugh maliciously at Waif's sentence. "I'm just here to decorate his garden. He says the blood makes the trees grow strong." A few more members

25

of the group, realizing that leaving while their leader was distracted was a viable option, beat their own hasty retreats. "Course, it's close to strangefruit harvesting time," Waif said, pointing towards the illusions of the hanged men in the trees. "We'll need a new ladder this year." Waif scanned the remaining five men and pointed at the tallest one. "Oh, his bones will make a *great* ladder. Nice and long."

"This is ridiculous," the leader said, but the tall man Waif had pointed out had reevaluated his life choices and decided he had urgent business elsewhere. "I've lived in Tallpines my entire life, how come I've never heard of this 'bone man' until today?"

Waif giggled, their eyes unnaturally wide and focused intently on the leader now. "You don't know about the bone man? He only comes when people decide to rob a tomb. That's what my parents did, they stole from the dead and the bone man punished them. I didn't do nothing, though, so the bone man took me to be his servant." While Waif was talking, Silas moved into the next phase of the illusion. He summoned strands of black smoke and shadow, and added voices whispering in a language which was perfectly normal but wasn't spoken within five hundred miles of Tallpines and would be completely unintelligible to the villagers. Silas had the smoke converge where the villagers were standing and begin pooling into a growing circle directly behind the ringleader.

When Silas had a bony hand reach up through the shadow, the remaining villagers immediately scattered into the woods. Because the leader was looking at Waif and there was nobody else to scare off, Silas fudged the next part of the illusion, creating a tall, skeletal figure standing in the center of the pool of shadow. It was vaguely humanoid but he modeled the head after an elk skull, complete with antlers. As a final touch, Silas draped the figure in a ragged old robe that looked to have been black once but had faded to gray with time.

"Oh, hi there, bone man!" Waif said cheerfully when the illusion was complete. "We's got another one for the harvest this year." The remaining villager turned around and Silas could only imagine the look on his face when he found a seven foot skeleton behind him.

"YES," the bone man said, "THIS ONE LOOKS READY FOR THE HARVEST," and reached a hand out towards the terrified villager, who fainted dead away. Waif poked the man a few times and then looked back towards where Silas was hiding.

"You didn't have to really kill him!"

"He's not dead," Silas said, emerging from his blind. "Didn't cast anything but some illusions, and maybe a little cantrip to make his fear stronger than any other emotions. Bundersnoot, anybody get their courage back?"

"Not yet." Bundersnoot jumped down from his observation post. "But they'll be back eventually."

"Right." With a wave of his staff, Silas dismissed all the illusions and the forest returned to its normal, non-haunted state. "Let's get back to the wagon and get moving. Waif, we can clean that makeup off when we've put enough distance between us and here. Bundersnoot, stop checking the man for snacks." Both Waif and Bundersnoot groaned but followed Silas deeper into the woods.

* * *

"There it is, Eynsworth Castle," Silas said as the castle finally came into view. Waif looked upon it with silent awe. *Monu-*

mental was a word that almost described the frost giant's castle. Almost. In the recent past, the castle had been one of dozens of nondescript mountains in the range. Through incredible effort an entire mountain peak had been transformed into the castle's keep. Great round towers rose from the slopes of the mountain, providing lookout posts for sentries and firing slits for archers. About halfway down the mountain, a curtain wall over sixty feet high encircled a plateau on the eastern ridge.

The gateway to the castle was flanked by two oval towers and massive crenelations twice as tall as a human topped the imposing edifice. The gate itself appeared to be made from enormous trees, old giants of the forest that had been saplings back when the world was small. A sentry from atop the tower noticed their arrival and hailed them. "Hello there! State your name and business!"

"I am the wizard Silas, I have guest-friendship with Jarl Brynjar of old and beg his hospitality."

"Enter, then. But know this, wizard, if you break the code of hospitality there shall be punishments severe." The sentry banged his spear on the roof of the tower and the gates slowly creaked open. Unperturbed, Silas led the wagon into the bailey of Eynsworth. A medium-sized village would have fit inside the castle's courtyard and it should have been bustling with activity. Instead there were a total of seven giants standing around with little better to do than watch the excitement. Including the giant on the gatehouse, it brought the total up to eight.

"Silas!" A giant with a gray beard down to his belt stepped forward and smiled. "It's good to see you, boy! How have you been?"

"Jarl Brynjar! Fair to middling, fair to middling. I come to

EYNSWORTH CASTLE

beg your hospitality and the use of your library."

Brynjar was tall for a giant, almost fourteen feet tall, but his shoulders were stooped with age. "I should have known, why else would a wizard come so far off the beaten path? Don't worry, Silas, you can pour over dusty old tomes to your heart's content. But first, we feast! What sort of host would I be if I did not lay out the best Eynsworth had to offer? Bergunn!" Brynjar began carefully climbing up the stairs towards the keep's entrance. "Bergunn! Have the boy bring a cask of the good mead from the cellar! We have any fresh meat in the castle?" One of the younger giants stepped forward and bowed courteously towards Silas.

"Please forgive our lord, Master Silas, there has been little of excitement of late. My name is Steinar and I am seneschal of the castle. I'll have one of the men stable your horse and I shall show you and your companions to your quarters."

* * *

The great hall of Eynsworth Castle had started as a cavern inside the mountain. Over the centuries, the giants had quarried stone from the heart of the mountain to build the curtain walls and towers of the castle and in the process created the hall. From a human perspective, colossal was simply too inadequate of a word. A host of two hundred giants could have fit comfortably within the halls confines, but with less than a dozen giants in residence it felt tragically empty.

"Have yourself some more deer!" Brynjar said, slicing a piece of meat off with a knife as long as Silas's arm and placing it on Silas's plate. "We've had wonderful hunting this season! Not much else to do this time of year. You there, Waif, was it? You still working on your first piece?"

Waif had grown up in the slums of Elade-voc and hadn't seen so much meat in one place in their entire life. They were still working through their first helping of food and nodded politely as they chewed. Bundersnoot, who was rabidly working on his *third* piece of deer, was mercifully silent. All three of them were seated on special chairs which brought them up to the height of the table. Brynjar had frequent enough human visitors that such accommodations were common.

"Forgive me, my lord," Silas said, "but I am curious as to the state of your hall. We came up through Tallpines and the villagers there said they hadn't heard from you for several years. The last time I came here your retinue was much greater." Six of the giants from the courtyard were seated at a trestle table close to Brynjar's high table with the seventh presumably still on sentry duty. A few female giants were sitting with those six, and every now and then, two more female giants would emerge from the entrance to the kitchen. In total, Silas guessed there couldn't be more than a score of residents in the entire castle.

Brynjar sat back and his face became contemplative. "I suppose the news hasn't gotten down to where you are yet. About fifteen years ago a war broke out further north between the frost giants and the fire giants. Saksi and my boys decided they wanted to go north and make a name for themselves. I tried to talk them out of it. Told them we had a good life down here and there was no sense getting involved in a squabble that didn't involve any of us. But once Saksi got an idea stuck in his head, he was determined to see it through."

Silas nodded. Saksi had been Brynjar's eldest son and per giant tradition, he would have inherited Eynsworth Castle when Brynjar died. Of all of his five sons, Saksi was the one Brynjar definitely indulged the most.

"Saksi talked all his brothers and about half my huscarls into following him, so they went up north to join the wars. They sent back word when they could, which was less often than I liked, but they were all hale and hearty until the battle of Frojfeld. That's… That's where Mimir died." Silas winced in sympathy. Mimir had probably been the wisest and most level-headed of Brynjar's five sons. Saksi would have been jarl after his father, but Mimir as his adviser would have kept the fiefdom on an even keel for centuries to come.

Brynjar paused, his eyes damp with tears for a pain that still hadn't fully healed. When he continued, Silas could feel the repressed sorrow in his voice. "They brought Mimir home and we interred him in the family crypt. I thought maybe now that they'd had a taste of war, Saksi and the others would be happy to stay at home. But Saksi, Snorri, Erik, even little Unferth, all of them had been changed. They wanted vengeance for their brother and swore a blood oath to extract all their pain and suffering from the fire giants with interest. They took almost all of my huscarls with them and marched back north. It's been six years now and I have no idea whether they're alive or dead, I've had no news. At this point, I must assume the worst."

"My friend, I am deeply sorry to hear of your loss," Silas said. "If you would like, I could attempt a scrying to see if I could find your sons."

Brynjar tried to look casual but his eyes betrayed his sudden interest. "If it would not be too much trouble for you, Master Silas. I would hate to impose upon your abilities as a wizard. I know you come here to pursue your own business, not indulge an old man."

"It would be the least I could do as recompense for your hospitality," Silas said. "A scrying would be very trivial work. In fact," he tossed a look at his charge and made eye contact with Waif, who had clearly been eavesdropping. Waif was suddenly intensely interested in the food remaining on their plate. "I think it would be an excellent opportunity to teach Waif some magic."

Waif swallowed the food they were working on and looked at Silas in surprise. "Me? But I don't know anything about any magic."

"Excellent," Silas said. "You don't come with any preconceived notions."

* * *

"Scrying is the attempt to discover the location of a specific person or object by a mage. The more well-known the subject of the scrying is to the mage, the more easily the scrying can be done. This is why it is almost impossible to scry for lost treasure, what with it being lost."

"But Master Silas, I'm not familiar with Saksi or Unferth or any of them," Waif said.

"Yes, and considering you are a complete novice, I could safely say it is impossible for you to find the location of any of Brynjar's sons on your own. But! We will be finding them with the help of Brynjar. My lord, if you would be so good."

Jarl Brynjar took out his dagger and carefully pricked the tip of his left ring finger. A small amount of blood beaded up and Brynjar squeezed the blood into a silver bowl Silas had prepared. The blood dispersed into the water Silas had filled the bowl with and became a pink cloud. "Thank you, my lord. Scrying can locate a person unknown to the scryer if the scryer has access to something which belonged to their target. In Brynjar we have the next best thing: the same blood."

Nervously, Waif stepped up to the bowl, it was only a slight exaggeration to say they could have taken a bath in it. "All right, so now what do I do?"

"Let's start with Saksi. Hold the name Saksi Brynjarson in your head." Silas took both of Waif's hands and placed them on either side of the bowl. "Now, simply ask the water to show you Saksi."

"That's it?"

"Trust me, if we didn't have a link through Brynjar this would be infinitely more complicated."

Waif closed their eyes and concentrated, thinking the name Saksi Brynjarson over and over. When they felt ready, they asked the water to show them Saksi. Waif opened their eyes to discover the bowl remained filled with blood-tinted water. "I don't think it worked."

"Not surprising," Silas said. "We've got three other names to try. Let's do Snorri Brynjarson."

Waif repeated the process again and again the bowl stubbornly remained utterly ordinary. The same result happened for Erik as well. "Master Silas, I don't think I can do a scrying at all. Maybe you should try."

"We still have Unferth Brynjarson. Let's give it one more try, okay?"

Waif nodded and repeated the process, convinced that absolutely nothing would continue to happen. They put Unferth's name in the forefront of their mind and then asked the water to please show them Unferth. And then, inexplicably, Waif started to feel like their teeth itched. There wasn't a better word for it, and running their tongue over their teeth didn't seem to help at all. Waif had barely enough time to process this before both Silas and Brynjar shouted with joy and surprise. Waif nearly jumped out of their skin in shock.

"You did it, Waif! I knew you had it in you!" Silas gave Waif an encouraging squeeze on the shoulder. "Open your eyes, child!"

Waif opened their eyes and looked at the bowl. The water glowed with gentle light and within the bowl Waif could see a young giant with the same nose and bushy eyebrows as Brynjar. He was seated in a hall much like Brynjar's own, unenthusiastically drinking from a mug of beer. "That's my boy, no doubt about it!" Brynjar said. "Praise to the ancestors, he's alive."

Silas put his hands on either side of the bowl and was able to manipulate the image, pulling away from Unferth and giving them a better view of where he was located. "Does any of this look familiar?" Silas asked. "Any symbols you recognize?"

"Yes! That's Halvard Hemmingson's black boar!" Brynjar pointed towards a banner hung prominently in the hall showing a fire-breathing boar trampling foes with impunity. "Halvard's only three hundred miles from here!" Brynjar's eyes brimmed with tears of joy. "Thank you, Silas. Thank you, Waif. I can bring my boy home."

* * *

Silas crouched on the roof of the bunkhouse in Tallpines, scanning the empty lot behind it. The lot was deserted for now, but no matter, he understood the benefit of patience. It was a moonless night and the evergreens surrounding Tallpines blocked the starlight, but Silas could see as if it were the middle of the day. Eventually someone stumbled from the bunkhouse and in the general direction of the outhouses. Silas smiled, his prey had finally revealed itself.

Silas leapt from the roof of the bunkhouse, landing with barely a whisper of sound behind the inebriated man. His prey was utterly oblivious to his approach, occupied with singing an off-key rendition of *Come Landlord Fill the Flowing Bowl* and slurring through the words. Silas did not hesitate and pounced. The man clumsily tried to resist Silas's assault but his drunken limbs refused to cooperate in his defense. In no time at all, Silas had pulled his head back, exposing his jugular.

Silas's fangs extended and he bit down, piercing the skin and tapping directly into the man's vein. The hot, salty taste of blood filled his mouth and his brain filled with ecstasy. Silas could feel himself growing stronger as he drank his victim's lifeblood, the fatigue draining away from him. It felt so incredibly right, why had he fought this for so long?

"Silas!"

Someone shouted his name and Silas looked up in confusion. But the lot behind the bunkhouse remained empty. He was about to begin drinking again when he heard his name again, shouted with greater urgency. And suddenly he felt a sharp pain in his chest? Like four sets of claws were digging into him? But that made no sense, he was alone.

"Silas!"

Silas woke with a start and found Bundersnoot standing on his chest, claws oh so slightly extended to get his attention. Bundersnoot had a concerned look on his face. "Come on, Silas, I need you to wake up. It's an emergency."

Silas groaned. "Bundersnoot, you had gods alone know how

much venison last night and an entire kitchen staff to coerce, wheedle, and beg. I'm not getting up to feed you."

"Oh, you stupid man, it's Waif!"

Groggily Silas pushed Bundersnoot off his chest and managed to sit up in bed. His brain scrambled about as it sorted between dreams and reality. He was pretty sure he hadn't attacked anyone in Tallpines, but he was still in that space between where things were not as clear cut. "Bundersnoot, did I go anywhere?"

"No? You've been here the entire time so far as I know. Why?"

"Bad dreams."

Bundersnoot looked up at Silas, concern evident on his face. "Well, tonight's the night for it, I guess. Waif's having a nightmare as well. I tried waking them but I didn't have any luck. I think they're revisiting the event with the Glutton."

A shiver ran down Silas's back at the mention of the name and any lingering sleepiness was pushed aside. "Take me to them," Silas said as he pulled on a robe and shoved his feet into shoes. Bundersnoot leapt down from the bed and headed towards a door on the far side of Silas's bedroom. Steinar had granted them use of a suite of rooms specially set aside for the use of human visitors to Eynsworth. Silas pushed the door open and found Waif tossing and turning in their bed, clearly troubled by nightmares. They were mumbling something, but Silas was unable to make out the words.

Bundersnoot immediately jumped onto the bed and carefully sat down on Waif's chest. "I'm trying to calm their mind but it's like fishing with your bare paws. Just when you think you've got the fish it wriggles away from you and jumps back into the stream. I need your help."

EYNSWORTH CASTLE

Silas pulled up a chair and sat down next to the bed. He took Waif's hand in one of his own and with his other hand he called upon the healing magic and held it six inches from Waif's head. Instantly Silas was hit with a wave of terror and he could hear the discordant music from that terrible night. "You're right, it's their memories from the Revelers incident. Let me do what I can." Silas concentrated and let his mind delicately touch Waif's, which appeared suddenly as a set of brilliant lights, energy flashing like lightning as different colors roiled and replaced each other.

Bundersnoot's spirit reached into Waif's mind as well, its warm orange glow slinking between the riots of colors. Where Bundersnoot went, the lightning decreased in frequency but they continued in strength and the colors continued to change rapidly. "I don't know enough healing magic to help with this," Silas said. "If I go in, I could end up hurting them."

"That's fine. I can calm their mind by myself, but I'm at the limits of my strength to do more. I need your brute strength I don't need your finesse. Can I use you as a reservoir?" One of the chief reasons wizards had familiars was to provide reservoirs of magical energy for particularly difficult or complicated spells. Less scrupulous wizards often saw their familiars only as sources of energy and would drain a familiar to death. But Silas's partnership with Bundersnoot was strong enough that either of them could act as a reservoir for the other.

"Ah, that I can do." Silas touched Bundersnoot and focused, channeling his own energy into Bundersnoot. He felt the pull as the energy left his body, went through Bundersnoot, and into Waif. He could see Bundersnoot's orange become brighter within Waif's mind and the lightning slowly abated. The colors continued to shift for some time afterward until it settled to a steady but extremely pale lavender. Bundersnoot waited a little bit longer before withdrawing his own energy back into himself.

"That should do it," Bundersnoot sighed with relief. "Thank you."

"I thought you said the nightmares were getting better," Silas said. "It's been weeks since you asked me for help."

"They *were* getting better," Bundersnoot said. "They haven't had a nightmare in a fortnight at least. Even after the ritual they didn't have nightmares this intense, I don't know what brought it up."

Silas frowned in concentration and considered an idea he wasn't fond of. "Bundersnoot, did you sense anything from me before you woke me up?"

Bundersnoot gently kneaded Waif's stomach and Waif's hand came down subconsciously to rub Bundersnoot's head. "I can't say for certain, my mind was on Waif. Why?"

"I was having a – possibly a nightmare, possibly something else before you woke me," Silas admitted. "I'm wondering if my mind might have affected Waif's in some way."

Bundersnoot twitched his whiskers in thought. "Definitely possible. I can't say if that's what happened tonight but now I know to be on the lookout for it. Anything in specific?"

Silas rubbed his arm, feeling the black scar underneath his sleeve. He considered glossing over the truth, but decided against it. If he couldn't trust his familiar, his oldest and closest companion, who else could he tell the truth to? "The vampire. Well, I *was* the vampire. It just felt so, so right to me. It scares me how *good* it felt. If we don't find what we're looking for here, I don't know where we'd go next."

Bundersnoot yawned and placed his head between his paws. "We'll cross that bridge when we come to it. Brynjar's library is large and poorly organized so you'll probably spend weeks searching until you're satisfied."

"I suppose you're right." Silas gave Bundersnoot a gentle scritch behind the ears and stood up. "Goodnight, Bundersnoot."

* * *

"I think Brynjar has more books than you do, Master Silas!" Waif stood at the entrance to the library, their mouth agape in astonishment.

"Probably, his family's been collecting longer than I have after all," Silas said. He whispered a word of power and pure white light emanated from the quartz crystal resting in the palm of his hand. Silas released it and it rose in the air, hovering two feet above Silas's head. The light illuminated the cavernous space, but only barely. A fan-vaulted ceiling disappeared into the gloom nearly thirty feet above them. Row after row of bookshelves, some reaching twenty feet high, stood in orderly ranks throughout the room.

Every shelf was crammed higgledy-piggledy with countless scrolls, codices, and other objects of interest. Silas's own library, a respectable collection of several hundred books, could have fit on just one of the massive bookcases. And he had scoured every single one of his own books, as well as any he could get his hands on in cosmopolitan Elade-voc, to find answers. He rubbed his arm nervously as the wound from the vampire twinged. If he couldn't find answers to his questions here, he had no idea where he could possibly go next.

The library was one of a few rooms built to accommodate both human and giant visitors within Eynsworth. Jarl Brynjar's family was unique among giants with their interest in books; most giants remained firmly dedicated to their oral traditions preserved by skalds. It was also furnished with reading desks available in sizes comfortable to both species, as well as staircases that spiraled at the end of each bookshelf, allowing humans to access a balcony attached halfway up each bookshelf. Silas walked over to a human-sized reading desk and was struck with a sudden thought. "Waif, do you know how to read?"

"No? Never really had a need to learn how in Bridgegate."

Silas hmmed thoughtfully. "I've been remiss in my duties, then." Silas dipped a pen in an inkwell, attempted to write on a slip of paper, and finding the ink had long ago since dried sighed in frustration and dug through his satchel until he could retrieve a pencil. He then carefully wrote some words on the paper and handed it to Waif. "Do you recognize any of these words?"

Waif frowned in concentration at the paper and gave it their best effort, but after a brief pause looked guiltily at Silas and said, "No. I know this is an O, and this is an X. And this is a D, I think."

"That's excellent!" Silas said encouragingly. "You recognize some letters already! That's very good!" Silas walked around so he was looking over Waif's shoulder and pointed at the words. "So these words say *Thirty Years of Exotic Diseases*. Don't worry about memorizing it right now, but that's one of the books I'm looking for. So we're going to look for a book that has these words on it. I don't know where it is, which is why I need your help finding it. So, where do you think we should look first?"

EYNSWORTH CASTLE

Waif looked over the library, taking in its grandeur and raised a hand, pointing towards and upper level off to the right. "Can we go up there?"

"Absolutely," Silas said, and took Waif by their other hand. "Let's go take a look."

Five hours later Bundersnoot padded into the library to find Silas and Waif sitting at one of the reading desks, a thick tome propped open in front of them. Silas was carefully reading to Waif, pointing with his finger to each word as he read. "Despite its dangerous horn, the Al-Miraj is an incredibly gentle creature and will only attack in self-defense. This has made the Al-Mirajs popular as pets and familiars among the Amastican nobility. Because they reproduce just as rapidly as normal hares, they are abundant on Serpent Island—"

"What does reproduce mean?" Waif asked.

"Make more of. Like when you put a boy cat and a girl cat together and you end up with kittens. Isn't that right, Bundersnoot?"

"Lunch is ready, if anyone was interested." Bundersnoot refused to recognize Silas's jab and maintained his composure. "Not that anyone cares if I starve to death, of course. All I get is abuse."

"Go ahead and have some lunch, I'll be along shortly," Silas said to Waif and they jumped down from their chair and ran towards the exit. "I assume that there is a reason you left the kitchen and its bounty of food?" He asked Bundersnoot.

"Genuinely interested to see how the research is going. I didn't realize you were doing a reading lesson." Bundersnoot jumped onto the reading desk and looked at the book. "Ah, Hugh of Fouilloy's bestiary."

"This *was* on my list of books to investigate, I've had no

luck finding Isidore the Barber-surgeon's *Thirty Years of Exotic Diseases* yet. Plus, I thought Waif would find a bestiary more interesting to read." Silas carefully turned over a large number of pages and went to the back of the bestiary until he came to the entry labeled "Vampires."

"Ah," Bundersnoot said, following along with Silas. "Still trying to find answers?"

Silas rolled up his sleeve and showed the black scar to Bundersnoot. "For whatever reason, Mistress Toquer did not describe this symptom in any of her books. Which makes me think she was never aware of Hugh's bestiary." Silas pointed to a passage.

The true vampire can infect victims with its curse through a number of ways. Its bite is the most common means of transmission, but any instance in which blood of the vampire mixes with blood of the victim will spread the vampire's curse. If a wound taken while fighting a vampire does not heal, or heals unusually, the victim will eventually turn. Despite rumors that there is a cure to the vampire curse, I have found no such evidence.

"Well, that definitely falls under 'heals unusually' as far as I'm concerned," Bundersnoot said. "Does it say how much time you have until the curse takes you?"

"A year, year and a half at most. Which gives us until next summer to try to cure this."

"Definitely doesn't give us a lot of leeway," Bundersnoot said. "Want me to take a look for Isidore while you take a break?"

"No, I can keep looking. It's bound to be around here somewhere. Nobody's come up here for years so it's bound to be here unless bookworms got to it first. Although I think it's too cold up here for book worms."

"Silas, listen to me." Bundersnoot sat on the bestiary and

looked directly into Silas's eyes. "You need to take a rest. Your brain will not function properly if you starve it of resources and you've been up here since morning. Now, are you going to go down and eat some lunch or am I going to have to sit on every book you try to read until you give up and take me downstairs to be fed?"

"You'd get bored eventually. Or fall asleep."

"That a bet?" Bundersnoot's green glass eyes bored into Silas and he finally looked away.

"All right, all right. I'm going to lunch! I hope you're satisfied!" Silas got up from the reading desk, rubbing his eyes, and walked towards the exit.

"And make sure to bring me something!" Bundersnoot called after him.

"No food in the library!"

* * *

Silas was running through the forest at night but he could see everything as clearly as if it was high noon. His prey was running, stumbling over roots and crashing through ferns as it tried to escape. He smiled, fangs extended, and jumped nimbly into the branches of the trees above. It should have been impossible for the slender pine boughs to take his weight, but the branches did not even bend as he stood upon them and leapt from one to the other with contemptuous ease. Soon, his prey was back in sight once again, stumbling into a creek.

If Silas had been a scent hunter, his prey's strategy of running up the creek to diffuse its scent might have mattered. But all it did was slow the prey down in a futile attempt to prevent its inevitable fate. Silas watched with amusement as his prey splashed through the creek, making enough noise to alert every predator within a mile. He could smell his prey's desperation, the thin hope it clung to that it might escape. It would make the blood taste all the sweeter when he brought his prey to ground and ripped their veins open.

He could smell that his prey was ripe, the hope almost overcoming the terror as it foolishly believed it had given him the slip. He glided down from the trees, landing directly in front of his prey. He laughed as he saw the hope drain from her eyes and be replaced with despair. She knelt, resigned to her fate, and exposed her neck.

"Silas!"

His fangs were set to pierce the supple flesh when he felt sharp pain in his own chest. Confused, he looked down, but no injury marred his perfect skin.

"Silas!"

Silas woke with a start to find Bundersnoot's green glass eyes looking directly into his own. "Hwah?" Silas mumbled, his mouth and brain operating independently of each other.

"You were having nightmares again. I tried soothing your mind but you kept pushing me out."

Silas gently lifted Bundersnoot from his chest and sat up, sleep still clouding his mind. "Was I here all the time? I didn't— I didn't go out into the forest or anything, did I?"

"I know for a fact you've been safely tucked in bed all night. Now talk."

"Same as last night but…different. I was a vampire again, hunting someone through the forest. My gods, I was *toying* with her. It was all a game to me and I was tormenting her on purpose. I saw her as a thing." Silas would have continued but

EYNSWORTH CASTLE

there was a knock at the door joining his chamber with Waif's.

"Master Silas, is it okay if I come in here for a bit?" Waif peered around the door, tousle-haired and sleepy-eyed. "I was having a bad dream and I woke up and I don't want to be alone right now."

"Oh, Waif, of course you can come in here." Silas got out of bed and put a dressing gown on, lighting a few candles with sparks of wytchfyre. Waif climbed up onto the bed and picked up Bundersnoot, cuddling him in their lap and giving him some belly rubs. Silas sat down in the room's chair. "What was your dream about?" Silas asked.

"I was back in that place," Waif said, not meeting Silas's eyes and focused entirely on petting Bundersnoot. "The scary place with the chanting and the voices and—" Waif paused, stifling a sob. "I don't wanna go back to that place. Do you have magic to make it stop?"

"Oh Waif, I'm so sorry." Overwhelmed by compassion, Silas stood up and hugged the child. "I'm so, so sorry this is happening to you. This should have never happened to you."

They sat there for a few minutes in silence, Bundersnoot and Silas doing their best to comfort Waif as they sniffled. Silas desperately wished he could fix the problem with a twist of his fingers or a few words of power to chase away the dreams. He was a wizard after all, magically fixing problems was what he was *supposed* to do.

"The mind is a delicate thing. Bundersnoot has some magic that he can use to help, but we don't have anything we can do to make the nightmares stop," Silas said as he sat back down and held one of Waif's hands in his own. "But you're not the only person to have nightmares after something like that happened. I used to adventure with a man named Gerald who had nightmares after we fought a lich."

Waif looked up, interested. "Was this the one you took the device from?"

"Yes, this was a very powerful sorcerer who had decided she wanted to live forever. So she took her life essence and put it in a phylactery, something very precious and very powerful. We had to storm her tower, which was woven with many powerful enchantments and guarded by a host of skeletons. Now Gerald was a knight, he had more courage than common sense, and he charged in with his sword hacking right and left at the skeletons. But it didn't matter how many heads he lopped off, the skeletons kept coming. So they surrounded him on his horse and pulled him onto the ground."

That particular incident was far more terrifying than Silas made it sound when he described it to Waif. There must have been several hundred skeletons that day when they'd fought the lich, and Gerald's horse was already spooked from the scent of dark magic. Silas had reason to suspect Gerald's foolhardy charge hadn't been entirely his fault. As the skeletons advanced on Gerald, Silas truly thought that was going to be the end of their adventuring careers.

"What happened then?" Waif asked, their eyes wide in fascination.

"It looked like the end for Gerald, he was going to be hacked to death by skeletons. But Narses, the elder Narses mind you, called up a mighty spell which called down the power of the sun and turned the skeletons to ash." Waif let out a small "wow" at this part of the story. "And so we rescued Gerald. But for a very long time afterwards he would have nightmares about the skeletons."

"And he was a knight?"

EYNSWORTH CASTLE

Silas nodded, remembering his old friend. "Yes, a great, big, strong man. He never let anybody know he was afraid of anything, but he still felt afraid a lot of the time. There's no weakness in being afraid, especially if it's something dangerous."

Honestly, Gerald's nightmares had been terrifying for everyone since he would often charge out of his bedroom swinging his great bronze sword at everyone. It was only the intervention of Bundersnoot and Narses's own familiar, Gingersnap, that had gotten Gerald to a point he didn't wake up and try to kill everyone. Even then Gerald's nightmares never truly went away, just got less intense with time.

Silas reached over and patted Waif on the shoulder. "What you experienced, young Waif, is one of the scariest things in the entire universe. So I think you're quite brave all on your own."

"Do you ever get scared?"

Silas frowned and thought, debating with himself what he should say. He was about to hedge when Bundersnoot interrupted. "Honesty is the best policy." He didn't even bother to open his eyes from his spot in Waif's lap.

"You're a vile traitor, you know that?" Bundersnoot didn't bother to respond, pretending to once again be soundly asleep. "We think part of the problem is I've also been having a lot of nightmares recently, and it might be affecting you. A little while before we rescued you, Bundersnoot and I fought a vampire in a village called Thornheath. We killed it, but not before it managed to wound me." Silas rolled his sleeve back and revealed the black scar on his arm, longer now than it had been. "That's why we've been looking for information, I'm hoping to find a cure."

47

Waif looked at his scar in fascination, reaching out and prodding it with their finger. "Wow. And you still have nightmares about fighting the vampire? It must have been really scary."

"It was," Silas admitted. "I was terrified the entire time. But what scares me even more is turning into a vampire."

Waif bit their lip and then looked up at Silas. "Is it okay if I stay here for the rest of the night? I feel safer here than by myself. When I lived in Bridgegate we never had our own beds. All us kids were piled in together so there was always somebody if one of us had a nightmare."

"I suppose so," Silas said, and yawned. "Goodness me, we better get some sleep while we can. We've got a big day of hunting through the library tomorrow. I've got a good feeling about some shelves I've been eyeing."

* * *

It in fact took several more days of searching but with Waif's help Silas was finally able to track down a copy of *Thirty Years of Exotic Diseases*. He brought the book over to one of the reading desks and carefully opened the tattered volume. "Let's see. Bloody Flux, Hegelian Chills, Rasping Fever, Spinovian Cough, Sweating Sickness, here we go, Vampirism." He laid the book out where Waif could see it as well and began to read.

Vampirism is spread through a contamination of the blood. If the blood of a vampire mixes with the blood of an individual, that individual will become afflicted with the curse. How quickly an individual will succumb to the curse seems to be determined by their overall health, but I have found applications of lunar caustic to the wound to be effective in delaying its onset. However, this is only a treatment, it is not a cure.

If a patient is afflicted with the curse of vampirism and is in danger of turning into one of the undead, there is only one cure that I know for certain to work. I have personally performed this cure two times but it has worked only once. First, you must obtain the tail of a manticore, for only its venom has sufficient potency to kill a person and ensure they shall not rise as vampire. Once the individual has expired, they must be resurrected by—

"Oh come on!" Silas exclaimed, stopping midway through the sentence. "There hasn't been one of those seen in—a hundred years at least!"

"What does it say?" Waif asked.

"I can't believe this." Silas did not explain further and stormed off, muttering under his breath.

* * *

The morning air was clear and cold, despite the bright sunshine. Jarl Brynjar and his retinue were gathered in Eynsworth's courtyard to see their visitors off. "Is there anything else we can do for you?" Brynjar asked. "I don't want people thinking I'm stingy when it comes to my guests."

"Your hospitality, as always goes unmatched. To be quite honest if we took any more I don't think we could make it down the mountain in one piece." Silas looked at the wagon and hoped that creaking sound wasn't the axles threatening to break. Jarl Brynjar had offered Silas his choice of books from the library and Silas had to keep his avarice firmly under control and limited himself to a mere twenty volumes. "I wish you the best of luck in finding Unferth and hope your quest succeeds."

Brynjar and his retainers had spent several days preparing for a journey north to Hemmingson's hall to try and bring Unferth home to Eynsworth. "Should only take us a week or so to get there if the weather stays good," Brynjar said. "And if he's moved on from there, I at least know where to start looking. Never has a guest given me a gift of such value, you have my thanks. Safe travels."

Bundersnoot waited until they had left the gates of Castle Eynsworth before giving in to his curiosity. "All right, Mister Mystical Wizard, I know for a fact you found a cure. Waif told me as much. Are you worried about fighting a manticore?"

"No," Silas said, keeping his eyes firmly fixed on the road before them. "I don't want to do it, no sane person would. But with the help of a Losanti huntress it should be reasonably achievable."

"Then it's about the second part of the cure. The part that you didn't tell Waif about."

Silas could feel Bundersnoot's gaze boring into him and he debated just distracting the cat with a treat. That might work in the short term but he doubted he would be able to fend off the cat's curiosity for forever. "It is. We have to go towards Tevioch and try to find a unicorn."

To that point Silas had never considered whether cats could laugh hysterically. All in all, he thought, it was a terrible time to find out

Elade-voc

"I'm coming! Good gods, what kind of service do you expect at this hour?" It was the middle of a dark winter night and Silas had been woken by a loud banging on the front door of his shop. He initially tried to ignore it, assuming whoever it was would get bored and move on to find warmth somewhere else, but apparently their determination was even greater than the cold. The insistent banging started again just as Silas reached the front door. He undid the locks and yanked it open in suitably dramatic fashion. "And what, in the Empress's holy name, is so damn important that you need to disturb me at three in the morning?"

Lady Gavreau, scion of the Gavreau merchant family, esteemed member of the City Council of Elade-voc, winner of the last election for Lady Mayor, the single most powerful person in the entire city, was grievously wounded and standing on Silas's doorstep. "Finally! I've been trying to rouse you for a good fifteen minutes." Lady Gavreau pushed her way into Silas's shop as if this was a perfectly ordinary thing to do, blood dripping from her mangled right arm. "How are you at healing magic?"

"Decent but it's not my specialization." Silas shut the door and frowned at the blood staining his floor. "Is there a reason you couldn't go to one of the temples at this hour?"

"No good, my enemies are watching the temples so they can finish me off. They don't know about you so I came here." Lady Gavreau walked into Silas's kitchen and sat down at the table. Silas lit several candles with a spark of wytchfyre and got a good look at Lady Gavreau's injuries. The good news was, aside from her right arm, she appeared to be in fine health. The bad news was that based on her right arm alone, she should be dead several times over. Large chunks of flesh had been torn out by the teeth of some creature, the wounds so deep that bone was visible. At least one artery had been severed, the probable source of the continual stream of blood.

Silas's stomach flip-flopped, first in perverse delight at the sight of so much blood, and then in revulsion. If he was going to cure his curse, he was going to have to leave for Losanti before winter snows closed the roads south. "Lady Gavreau, please pardon my asking, but how on earth are you still alive?"

"Healing potions," Lady Gavreau said, and she pulled a vial filled with a softly glowing red tincture from her belt. She pulled the cork open with her teeth and spat it onto the table before downing the potion. The potion helped a little, knitting together flesh that existed but unable to work with material that wasn't there. "I know, I would be dead several times over without them."

Silas started boiling some water and put a clean towel down on the table before examining Lady Gavreau's arm. "I'll be honest, the easiest way to fix this would be amputation at the shoulder."

"Not an option." Her response was immediate and firm. "If I wanted to amputate, I could do it myself."

"Never make my life easy, do you?" Silas muttered. "Bundersnoot! Get down here! And find Waif while you're at it!" Silas started with preliminary stabilizing magics to ensure that his patient wouldn't die in his kitchen, which gods alone knew would lead to all manner of problems he didn't need. He started by encouraging the artery to grow, gently coaxing it to remember the pathway it took before it had been ripped apart. With the artery rejoined Gavreau stood a much better chance of surviving the night.

Bleary-eyed, Silas looked up and saw Waif and Bundersnoot waiting expectantly. "Bundersnoot, I need you to keep her stable while I gather materials." Bundersnoot blinked in assent and jumped into Gavreau's lap, working his unique magic. "Waif, you get that kettle boiling."

Waif headed over to the hearth and stirred the coals into life, adding fresh wood to the fire. Silas went around the kitchen pulling down jars of ingredients and lining them up on the table. Finally he got a mortar and pestle and started grinding components together. "Sage, soldier's woundwort, hyssop, rosemary, add that together with some honey. Where did we put the honey?"

"Top shelf of the pantry," Bundersnoot answered. Silas fetched the honey down and began mixing it and the herbs together in a separate bowl.

"What are you making?" Waif asked.

"It's a poultice to prevent blood poisoning from setting in," Silas explained. "No sense in us putting her arm back together if she succumbs to a fever a few days later. This is always very, very important when you're taking care of wounds, young Waif. How's that water coming along?"

"Almost boiling."

"Good, pour a little bit of the water in that mug and then

when the rest has been a rolling boil for two minutes, let me know."

"What's the mug for?" Lady Gavreau asked.

"This? Oh this is for me. I've got several hours of work ahead of me and if you want me to be lucid I'm going to need stimulants." Silas dipped a bag of *mostly* tea in the mug and let it steep. "Bundersnoot, let's take a look at that arm again."

* * *

It took several hours of hard work but Silas managed to get Lady Gavreau's arm back to a fit enough state where natural healing could take over. Exhausted, he collapsed into a kitchen chair across from her as she examined her arm. "You have my thanks, Master Silas. I shall make sure you receive adequate recompense for your services this night."

"Don't poke at it, the skin's still healing. You could still get blood poisoning and then where would we be?" Lady Gavreau pulled her left hand away and placed it back on the table as Silas downed the remainder of some lukewarm tea. Waif was safely tucked back into bed upstairs, leaving the adults free to talk.

"I heard about Deepwater from the Comtesse d'Souillard," Gavreau said, flexing her right arm experimentally. "She was impressed you were able to take down a war construct by yourself, although disappointed she wasn't able to salvage it. Word is the Empress is offering hefty rewards for even broken war constructs."

"If I run into another one, I'll try to not leave it at the bottom of a lake. Did she say if there were any survivors?"

"Forty or fifty souls, although there are just as many still missing. There was enough of a harvest left for them to start rebuilding."

Silas felt a small spark of hope. At least his efforts hadn't all been for naught. However he didn't let the past distract him for long. "What I want to know is how your arm got so mangled in the first place. I assume this has something to do with city politics?"

"My dear wizard, I cannot sneeze without it having an affect on city politics. I do not know who precisely is behind this attack. It could be some remnant of the Larousse family attempting to get vengeance for Eugénie or it could be the Rouselles attempting to clear the board."

"Zéphyrine Landfall, the Imperial Trade Factor," Bundersnoot mumbled, not bothering to open his eyes from his place in Gavreau's lap.

"What?" Both Silas and Gavreau looked at him in surprise and Bundersnoot blinked his green eyes open.

"Zéphyrine wants to reassert Amastican hegemony over Elade-voc to curry favor with her Cascade cousins, which is why she was bankrolling the Rouselles in the last election. Lucienne Rouselle is basically her puppet. Honestly, Charlène, I don't know why you're surprised by this."

"Delegate Landfall's ambitions to return Elade-voc are well known to me, if only because she besieges my office every week trying to get me to make this or that concession favorable to the empire." Gavreau tilted her head and blinked, looking not unlike Bundersnoot in that particular moment. "But the Rouselles? Really? She took a look at the families of Elade-voc and settled on the Rouselles?"

"As I understand it, their lack of creative thinking endeared them to her initially but she has been reevaluating that decision as of late." Bundersnoot yawned and closed his eyes again. At one point the Rouselles had been lead by matriarchs just as quick-witted, devious, and ruthless as any of the merchant houses in Elade-voc. That is how they became rich, after all. But their current wealth was due to inertia more than anything else and nobody had seen the Rouselles as serious players in two generations. "But the loans she took out to fund the Rouselles come due in a few weeks and she's gotten desperate. Which is probably why she set that trap with the mimics for you."

"SHE DID WHAT?!" Lady Gavreau attempted to jump out of her chair but there was a thrum of magical energy and Silas could feel his teeth tingle as Bundersnoot exerted downward force on Lady Gavreau. She struggled against Bundersnoot's power but was unable to overcome it.

"Your ladyship, please, you're liable to strain something and we just put you back together." Silas stepped over to the hearth and started warming more water for tea. "Bundersnoot, how exactly did you find all of this out in the first place?"

"Delegate Landfall's familiar, Ambassador. He's not terribly bright but he makes up for it in raw magical ability. He likes to impress the lady cats by talking about her secret plans and then the lady cats talk to everyone else. Honestly, if Delegate Landfall knew she'd probably have had him gelded ages ago."

"And the mimics, where did they come from?" Gavreau asked.

"I imagine she summoned them in at some point. It's not hard, even Silas could summon mimics if he really wanted to."

"Well, there are two ways of doing it, but which one is simpler depends on which disciplines are your specialization." Silas launched into a technical explanation with some eagerness.

It had been some time since he had problems of the non-vampiric curse variety. "Summoning a mimic from the Land of Fae is fairly straightforward but you have to have a strong summoning circle or it will attempt to eat you as soon as it arrives. Enchanting a mimic is considerably more difficult but the mimic is far more obedient when the process is complete. It really depends—"

"Silas," Bundersnoot interrupted before it turned into a full dissertation.

"Right, right, not important right now. Lady Gavreau, where exactly did you encounter these mimics?"

"I was inspecting a townhouse that I am interested in purchasing, it's always a sound decision to invest in real estate."

"In the middle of the night?" Silas asked, skeptically.

Gavreau waved this question away with frustration. "I have a very, *very* busy schedule as mayor. Most of my business affairs can be left to my factors, but if I'm going to lay out the money for a building I want to know what I'm getting. Although in hindsight, the owner's eagerness to let me examine it well after dark probably should have been a warning.

"Anyway, so I turn up with two city guards and this wizened old woman says she's the caretaker and lets me into the house. We go down into the cellar and I see this large chest sitting out in the middle of the floor—" Gavreau's story was cut off as Silas let out a frustrated groan.

"Why, by the Eight Schools and the Empress's holy name, do they *always* make it a chest? It could be literally *any* piece of furniture but it's always a chest! Every time!"

"Yes, before I was rudely interrupted, I was going to say that the chest proceeded to attack us, killed both of my guards, and mauled me rather badly. Of the caretaker there was no sign.

Fortunately I was able to escape and find you awake. So I take it you have extensive experience dealing with mimics, Master Silas?"

"Unfortunately," Silas admitted. "I can't remember how many mimics I defeated in my adventuring days, but it must have been hundreds."

"Excellent. Then you'll have no difficulty defeating this mimic while I plot my revenge against Delegate Landfall."

Silas had to work *very* hard to suppress his urge to swear violently.

* * *

From across the street, the townhouse looked perfectly normal. It was built in the newer style, utilizing the yellow bricks that had become available from the new factory upriver. It expressed wealth in a way that was tasteful and understated. But there were no other signs the building was occupied. The short path from the front door to the street remained covered in snow, something one of the many servants of an occupied house of this class would have done as soon as it was daylight. The leaded-glass windows, showcasing the owner's ability to purchase large amounts of glass and to let in natural light, were covered with thick curtains. If anybody was home, they didn't want the outside world to know it.

Silas hmmed and rested his chin on the end of his staff. "At least one mimic, but how many other surprises are in there? It could be an entire set of booby-traps just to get Lady Gavreau."

"Why are we doing this?" Waif asked, stamping their feet to bring some warmth back into their toes. "I understand the part where she's the mayor and we should probably do as she asks, but why are we tackling *this?*" Waif pointed towards the house.

"First, because it will be an excellent education for you, young Waif. It is never too early to teach someone about the dangers of mimics. Second, while it would be fairly simple for Lady Gavreau to send some of her armed retainers to go in, slaughter any mimics they found, and trash the place, she wants a lighter touch that may be able to find evidence of Delegate Landfall's involvement. Ah, here he comes."

Bundersnoot was an easily seen flash of orange among the whites and grays of the snow, which was rapidly turning to slush as Elade-voc came awake for the day. He carefully picked his way through the street, avoiding lumps of dubious origin, and joined them. "Talked to the neighborhood cats like you asked, they confirmed there's nobody inside. Fizzgig said she saw Lady Gavreau leave last night and the caretaker left about an hour afterwards. Between her, Napkin, and Broomstick they've seen nobody come in or out of the place since then."

"Still leaves us with one mimic to deal with. All right." Silas began striding confidently towards the house, forcing the other two to follow. "First lesson, young Waif—"

"You've taught me things before."

"Quiet, you. First lesson *of the day*: if you act like you're supposed to be somewhere nine times out of ten people will assume you belong there. Which is why we are walking towards this house like we own the place rather than skulking about like common burglars." Silas stopped only long enough to open the gate, pushing against the accumulated snow, and entering the tiny garden. There was about five feet of space between the fence at the curb of the street and the entrance of the house. Barely enough room to grow anything, but within the walls of Elade-voc, where space was at a premium and buildings rose cheek-by-jowl in a competition for air and light, setting even this much land aside was a statement of wealth.

They came to the varnished wood door and Silas attempted the bronze latch. He could feel it jiggle, but the door remained firmly locked.

"Do we have to break in?" Waif asked.

"Yes and no," Silas answered. "What I'm about to do is, under the laws of the city, *technically* breaking and entering. However we're not going to do anything so crass as break the door down. We're going to try a very simple spell." Silas shook his hands out of the sleeves of his robe and made some mystical gestures in the air before finally saying, "Excuse me, door, we need to get in." There was a series of five audible knocks, a pause, two more knocks, and then the lock thunked open and the door swung open an inch.

"That's it?" Waif asked.

"Most magic involves asking things for their cooperation, the secret lies in knowing *how* to ask." Silas pushed the door open and Bundersnoot darted inside ahead of them. The foyer of the house had a checkerboard floor made of tiles of red and white marble and dark oak paneling, all of which had been installed at considerable expense. Bundersnoot was already sniffing at a streak of blood that had not been cleaned from the floor.

"I *assume* this is Lady Gavreau's, it's too dry for me to be sure." Bundersnoot made a face. "I can smell the mimic, though. That, or somebody has kept a bunch of spoiled meat somewhere in the house."

"She said they found the mimic in the cellar, let's start our search there." Silas walked towards an empty dining room, the only clue of its use being the sideboard integrated into the room's wall. He stepped into the middle of the room and turned around slowly, examining the walls of the room in turn. "Ah, they hid it, very clever. But then again, we don't like knowing our servants exist now do we? Let's see, the front of the house is that way so—"

"What is he doing now?" Waif whispered to Bundersnoot.

"As much as they'd like to pretend servants don't exist, the wealthy still need their food to make its way from the kitchen to the dining room. So there should be some sort of servants' passage, he's just trying to find it."

"Ah, there we go!" Silas strode towards one corner of the room and pressed a piece of the wood paneling. Part of the wall swung aside to reveal a short passage with blood splattered across the floor. "Definitely on the right path." Silas stepped through and entered the kitchen, which, in contrast to the front of the house, was entirely utilitarian in its decoration. The walls were whitewashed to help reflect light from the narrow windows and the floor was a porous tile that was easy to scrub clean, a task the caretaker had not bothered with since the trail of blood remained on the tiles leading directly to the cellar.

"Yep, definitely a mimic down there," Bundersnoot said as he gingerly stepped over the kitchen tiles. "Smells like rotten meat and cedar wood."

"Are you sure? I can't smell anything," Waif said.

"It's subtle, most humans probably wouldn't be able to sense it," Bundersnoot explained. "Part of the benefits of having an animal companion. Although..." Bundersnoot frowned and closed his eyes, taking deep sniffs of the air. "Definitely one in the cellar but I feel like..."

"At least it hasn't moved," Silas said. "Everyone stay close, and Waif, don't touch *anything*." The stairs leading down into the cellar were wide and solidly built, meant to make the lives of the servants just a little bit easier. Silas summoned a small ball of white light and they could see several large bins meant to hold staple crops, as well as extensive shelves for preserved foods. And in the center of the room, standing all by itself, was a treasure chest.

Silas let out a very long, very tired sigh. "All right, Waif. It is time for me, in the parlance of the my late grandfather, to learn you something. In theory, mimics are the perfect ambush monsters. Capable of disguising themselves in any environment, they could be any number of ordinary objects. However, for whatever reason the Empress alone knows, nine times out of ten mimics take the form of treasure chests thus making them the most obvious of traps."

"Plus they smell like rotten meat," Bundersnoot added.

"Yes, dental hygiene seems to be low on a mimic's list of priorities."

"But why is it such an obvious trap?" Waif asked. "It seems perfectly innocuous to me."

"Waif, I spent the better part of fifty years adventuring across the length and breadth of this good green earth. I have raided temples, delved dungeons, briefly fought in a war, and have had tea with a rather sociable dragon. *Never* in any of those fifty years have I encountered a treasure chest that wasn't a mimic."

"Then why do we call them treasure chests?" Waif asked.

"That is a hotly debated philosophical question among magical practitioners the world over. Last I checked, the hypothesis seems to be that mimics have some ability to influence minds of the unwary and make them think the mimics are filled with treasure. Something that makes people take a look at mimics and say, 'Oh, that's a treasure chest! There's treasure inside of there!' Of course as the old saying goes the plural of wizard is argument so some people disagree whether from deeply held convictions or just to be contrary."

"Silas," Bundersnoot warned. "I think the you-know-what is starting to get suspicious." It was hard to see in the confines of the cellar but there was the definite suggestion of a large, purple tongue running across the lid in anticipation.

"Ah, right. The other main thing to remember about mimics, young Waif, is that they are incredibly fireproof. Which is why it's important we- LIGHTNING BOLT!" Without warning Silas thrust out his hand and an arc of blue-white lightning shot directly into the center of the treasure chest. The mimic squealed in pain and shock, jumping nearly a foot into the air. It hopped around, making wounded animal noises as Silas shocked it again with another bolt of lightning and left a large, blackened hole in the center of the mimic. It squealed like a stuck pig and collapsed into a pile of slowly dissolving flesh.

"It appears that Delegate Landfall is an expert at summoning creatures from the Land of the Fae, then. If she had created an enchanted creature, we would be looking at some broken wood and bronze. Summoned creatures tend to turn into…" Silas walked over and gently prodded the pile of gray goop with the end of his staff, "…this."

"What is it?" Waif asked.

"I'm not entirely sure," Silas admitted. "I can do summonings, I have a chamber for it back in the shop, but I find creatures from the Land of the Fae unpleasant to work with. Although, I imagine if someone pulled me into the Land of the Fae against my will, I wouldn't exactly be happy either." The gray goop was rapidly disappearing through the dirt floor of the cellar and was gone within a matter of moments. "And just like that, no evidence that there was ever a mimic. Perfect deniability for Delegate Landfall."

"Silas, something's wrong," Bundersnoot said as he lashed his tail back and forth. "I'm still smelling a mimic somewhere in the house."

"Another one? Where?"

"I don't *know*! Why don't we look around for another treasure chest or something?" Bundersnoot was pacing the breadth of the cellar, investigating its shadowed corners. Bundersnoot was about to leap onto a set of shelves when Silas had a terrifying thought.

"Bundersnoot, don't!" But it was too late, Bundersnoot had already jumped into the air and landed gently on one of the shelves.

"What?" Bundersnoot asked, turning around and looking at Silas quizzically.

"Oh thank the gods," Silas said, hand to his chest as he took a deep breath. "I had a moment where I thought the shelves might be a mimic."

"Trust me, if these shelves were a mimic I would have smelled it. I don't think it's down here in the cellar, but it's *somewhere* in the house."

Silas groaned. "All right, I guess we'll be searching the house room by room then. Waif, remember, don't touch *anything*."

"But if they always disguise themselves as a treasure chest, then why-"

"Not *always,* just a solid nine times out of ten," Silas said. "And that is another important lesson about survival. A little bit of knowledge can be more dangerous than no knowledge at all." They made their way up the stairs of the cellar back into the kitchen and Silas extinguished the sphere of light. "I told you a fact about mimics, which you extrapolated into knowledge about *all* mimics. But there is a chance this other mimic is slightly more intelligent."

The kitchen remained as it was before, with none of the heavy pieces of furniture having mysteriously moved since they last left the room. Bundersnoot slowly walked a circuit of the room, inspecting the furniture and occasionally stopping to take deep sniffs. He sneezed and twitched his whiskers in irritation. "The mimic isn't in here, but this room hasn't been dusted in quite some time. I think I can hear mice in the walls too. If Lady Gavreau still wants to buy this house after all this, I'd recommend she reconsider."

"I'm sure she'd be greatly appreciative of your input," Silas said, pushing his way through the servants' passage into the dining room. "But that's not our concern right now." They continued slowly through the rooms of the house one by one, Bundersnoot and Silas investigating every piece of furniture draped in white dust covers. Waif stayed close to Silas, mindful of his advice and endeavoring to give all pieces of furniture a wide berth. But annoyingly, of the other mimic they could find no trace.

"I think it's upstairs," Bundersnoot said. "Which makes a certain kind of sense, I suppose. If you want to lure someone into a trap better to have it where a passerby wouldn't be able to see it easily."

"I dislike how deviously your mind works sometimes, Bundersnoot," Silas said.

"I'm a cat, can you blame me?" Silas let that question go

unanswered. Cautiously they climbed the grand wooden staircase to the upper floors of the house. The second floor consisted of bedchambers for the family owning the house, each room having large windows which were, admittedly, made of inferior glass than what was used on the first floor. Most of the rooms were empty, occasionally containing either an abandoned washstand or a rickety chair, none of which gave off the characteristic stench of rotten meat. Finally, they entered the master chamber, a large room set aside for the owner of the house and her spouse. This room contained two pieces of furniture: a large feather bed, so large it must have been brought into the room in pieces, and at the foot of the bed, a single treasure chest.

Without any hesitation or warning, Silas let loose with a bolt of lightning, striking the treasure chest directly in the center and blasting a large, blackened hole in the center of the chest, which...remained where it was. The chest continued to sit there, nothing more than a piece of very mundane and now very damaged furniture. "Well, that's a surprise," Silas admitted. "Maybe the mimic's upstairs in the servants' quarters? It would make sense to hide it even further up in the— OH MY GODS— " This last part was shouted in response to the feather bed shifting itself, shaking like a lumbering animal as it stalked on its four legs towards the three of them.

"Waif! Get behind me! Run!" Inwardly Silas was cursing himself for his overconfidence. As an experienced wizard he should have known not to take such a stupid risk, but it was too late now. In a panic, they fled into the hallway and towards the staircase. Waif and Bundersnoot ran down the stairs at full tilt while Silas stopped to prepare a spell. His courage faltered when he saw the bed squeeze through the doorway, unimpeded by the narrowness of the door, and emerge into the hallway.

A mouth that should not have been on *any* piece of furniture yawned out from the footboard of the bed, revealing a massive purple tongue and teeth as long as Silas's forearm. He summoned more lightning but it seemed only to enrage the creature as it roared in anger. Silas barely had time to duck into another room as it charged forwards to trample him beneath its four wooden legs. The mimic, unable to react in time, continued down the hallway before screeching to a halt, wood scraping against wood.

Silas stepped into the hallway again, keeping an eye on the mimic as it turned around in the confined space. "Bundersnoot!" Silas shouted down the stairs. "I'm going to try pulling a Forsberg on this one. Get the front door open and see if you can lure it outside."

"A Forsberg? What in the Empress's name are you talking about— Oh right, a Forsberg! Waif, stick close to me, things are about to get messy!" Silas heard them open the door of the house and flee into the drifts of snow. Silas turned his attention to the spell, summoning forth a thin layer of a slick substance. It covered the entirety of the stairs and part of the landing at the top of the stairs as well. He finished setting up for his plan just in time for the mimic to finally to turn itself around and begin its charge.

Nimbly, Silas managed to step aside once again, dodging like a gladiator avoiding a lion—with mere inches to spare. The mimic tried to halt its charge, the legs leaving long scrapes on the floor, but its inertia led it into Silas's trap. It slipped, unable to gain purchase thanks to Silas's spell, and fell down the stairs, where it rapidly gained speed and whooshed through the foyer before finally crashing into the open door frame.

Carefully, Silas stepped to the top of the stairs, avoiding his own trap, and surveyed the damage. The mimic was wedged into the doorway of the house, half inside and half outside. It struggled and tried to squeeze its way back into the house, the frame of the bed rippling like the muscles of an animal. Silas sent another bolt of lightning into the mimic and this time, it took. It squealed in pain and aggravation, managing to pop through the doorway and into the garden outside. Bundersnoot immediately pounced on the mimic, scratching at its legs with his claws while managing to avoid being trampled by the increasingly frustrated monster.

The mimic let out a final scream of pain and jumped over the waist-high wall separating the garden from the street, bowling over a number of curious onlookers in its escape. It scrabbled through the snow, leaving a trail of confused and frightened people in its wake. "Should we go after it?" Waif asked, brushing snow off themselves and gawping at the chaos.

"No, at this point it's going to run back to its mistress and it'll be Delegate Landfall's problem," Silas said, surveying the damage to the house. The front door would be in desperate need of repair, based on the deep gouges cut into the doorjamb, but the rest of the house had survived mostly intact. A few hours of good carpentry work and it would be like it had never happened. "Come on, Bundersnoot, let's sweep the house and make sure there are no other mimics."

"But I haven't had breakfast yet!" Bundersnoot protested. "You can't make me work under these conditions! This is cruel, unusual, and just plain not fair."

"I haven't had breakfast yet either." Silas was, in fact, running on a rapidly diminishing reserve of borrowed energy from the tea he had drunk earlier. "Let's just do a final sweep and then I'll see about getting you some pulled chicken for breakfast."

"If you think you can just bribe me with chicken...you're absolutely right," Bundersnoot said, and he trotted back into the townhouse to check for mimics.

"Waif, how would you like to learn how to do a detection spell?" Silas said, as he shepherded his ward back into the townhouse. "It's a little more complicated than scrying but it's a very similar, very basic magic."

"I get to learn more magic?" Waif asked, excitement shining in their eyes and Silas chuckled, remembering his own excitement at that age.

"Sure thing, kid, you've earned it."

* * *

"You released a mimic into the streets of Elade-voc, where it terrorized the people of Lindenwood, did an as-of-yet uncounted number of damages to the Northgate Market *and* the Merchants Quarter, and then stampeded across the Gold Bridge into the Temple District before being slain by members of the city garrison. Six of whom have serious injuries." Lady Gavreau's nostrils flared in displeasure. "I asked you to handle this problem quietly and you put half the city in a panic!"

"Just out of curiosity, whose home did the city garrison stop the mimic outside of?" Bundersnoot asked, blinking nonchalantly from his place in Silas's lap.

"It was, in fact, the residence of Delegate Landfall," Lady Gavreau admitted grudgingly. "And before you ask, yes, I am already suggesting to Zéphyrine that it may be in her best interests to resign her post here. After all, someone appears to have tried assassinating her with a mimic, who knows what they might attempt next?"

"And her creditors?" Bundersnoot asked.

"Sadly learning that sometimes, even an Imperial Trade Delegate's word isn't as good as gold."

"So aside from some property damage, news the city will talk about for another three months, and a few injuries, I think you could call this a success. A game well played, Your Ladyship." Bundersnoot closed his eyes and kneaded Silas's thigh gently.

"What about you, wizard? You have any opinions to offer?"

"Oh, I let Bundersnoot handle politics, he's much better at it than I am," Silas said. "I simply haven't the head for it. Although that does come to our matter of payment for services rendered."

"I suppose it was too much to expect you to act out of a sense of civic patriotism."

"You got blood all over my floors and I lost a good night's sleep saving your life, Lady Gavreau. At my age, I'm not sure how many good nights sleep I have left. However, I may offer a discount if you are willing to do me a favor."

"Perhaps." Lady Gavreau leaned back in her chair and looked at Silas across her desk. "What sort of favor are you interested in?"

"I'd like to find Waif's parents, if they're still alive. Sadly, my connections in the city are not up to the task." He looked down at Bundersnoot and frowned. "But I would appreciate it if we could at least locate them." Silas had meant to spend more time looking for Waif's parents but his quest for a cure had taken him far from home and it felt irresponsible to leave Waif behind. Now he had half a year, maybe a little longer, to try to save himself and if that failed *someone* was going to have to take care of Waif.

"That might take some time," Lady Gavreau said. "Bridgegate is overflowing with the destitute and desperate. Do you have names and descriptions?"

"Waif says their mother had the same green eyes as they do and everyone said they had their father's chin, but beyond that it could be anyone in the city. No surname to my knowledge but the father's given name is Grégor."

"I'll have my agents stir the pot and see what floats to the top, but that will take time."

"Unfortunately I have no time to wait, we are heading south for Losanti in a matter of days on personal business."

"Losanti? Your business takes you very far afield, Master Silas. Very well." Lady Gavreau reached across her desk and spread a sheet of paper on her blotter. She carefully wrote on the paper, poured red sealing wax on the paper, and impressed it with her signet ring. Satisfied, she handed the paper over to Silas. "That is a letter of credit which most merchants south of here should honor. At least as far as the Oya River. Do you know when you will return?"

Silas felt his arm twinge and resisted the urge to rub it. Hopefully he'd be able to find the necessary components in time. Hopefully. "I imagine I may be gone for quite some time."

Losanti

A rare break in the clouds allowed the sun to reflect on the waters of the Oya River. Even during the rainy season, the Oya was shallow enough here just above the Third Cataract that they could walk across into the land of the Losanti. Silas had left their wagon at the imperial fort, the last outpost of Amastican authority and the end of the great road that ran all the way back to Elade-voc. Going forward into the grasslands the Losanti called their home, the wagon would have been more a hindrance than a help. Hopefully, despite the foul weather, they would be able to find a manticore without too much difficulty.

Waif was struggling to remain on top of their horse and Silas suspected it was only the gentle encouragement of Bundersnoot that was keeping the horse from attempting to buck both of them off. Waif attempted to re-tie the colorful wrap draped around their torso and gave a sound of frustration. "Why do I need to dress like a girl anyway?" Waif complained. "I'm not a girl!"

"I know," Silas said. "But the Losanti won't listen to a boy."

"I'm not a boy either."

"I know, but that's not important right now. The Losanti are *extremely* matriarchal and I am very obviously male, so I need you to pretend to be my daughter. It's just until we find a manticore and get out of here."

Waif gave up trying to rearrange their clothing and took up the horse's reins. "Is that why you look like you're dressed up like that?" Silas was dressed head to toe in black robes that covered almost every inch of his skin, leaving only his hands visible. Even Silas's face was covered, with only a small eye-slit allowing Silas to peer out at the world.

"Unfortunately, yes. The Losanti believe that men are too violent and emotional to be trusted with anything other than warfare and manual labor. This means that *all* men, regardless of age, need to have a female family member who is responsible for them in some capacity. Hence why you are pretending to be my daughter."

"But we're not from here, can't we just dress normally?" Waif protested.

"Waif, I'm going to give you a bit of very valuable advice I have learned from my years traveling from place to place: it's that if you honor the customs and traditions of the local people they're more willing to help you. We *could* try to defeat a manticore on our own, but are you prepared to face down a creature twice the size of a lion with a venom so potent it can kill an elephant in a matter of seconds?"

"Not really," Waif admitted.

"And neither am I," Bundersnoot chimed in. "Let's get moving and find the next village so I can get some food. I'm starving."

"Bundersnoot, you *just* ate at the fort." Silas said. "How could you *possibly* be hungry again?"

"You call that a meal? One itty-bitty fish barely enough to whet my appetite? This is a coordinated campaign of torture by the two of you. I shall waste away to nothing at this rate."

"Here, have some jerky." Waif pulled a strip of dried meat out of their saddlebag and offered it to Bundersnoot. He wrinkled his nose in disgust, then thought better and chomped greedily on the snack. The sky darkened and low, heavy clouds that threatened rain covered the sun.

"We better get going, we've been fortunate so far in the weather but I doubt that will last. Come on, the commander of the fort garrison said there was a Losanti village just a few miles south of here." Silas gently encouraged his mare forward and she began following the dirt trail through the grasses of the savanna. A few lonely acacia trees on the horizon were the only break in the sea of grasses surrounding them. Silas hoped this was the right way to find the Losanti village or they might wander around for gods alone knew how long.

An hour into their journey south, the clouds finally opened and they were pelted with a raging downpour. The dirt trail quickly turned into a muddy morass and any progress they were making slowed to a crawl. Silas and Waif both pulled out heavy rain cloaks of waxed cloth and draped them over their bodies, trying to keep themselves mostly dry, and Bundersnoot quickly huddled under Waif's cloak. Silas had to stand directly next to Waif and almost shout at the top of his voice to be heard over the sound of the rain.

"It's about midday right now, we've got several more hours of daylight left. We're going to stop there for an hour and give the horses a rest." Silas pointed towards a grove of trees a little ways ahead, barely visible through the downpour. "I want to keep pushing ahead for as long as we can. Hopefully we'll find a good campsite before it starts getting dark."

"I vote we stay there," Bundersnoot said, peering out from

beneath Waif's cloak. "It's at least *some* sort of shelter. We can wait until the rain lets up."

"We can pray that the rain will let up, but there's no guarantee it will. You know this as well as I do."

"I don't know why I bother staying your familiar," Bundersnoot complained. "Insufficient food, intolerable working conditions, irregular hours. I bet not even Delegate Landfall treated her familiar like this!" Silas paid Bundersnoot's grousing no mind and led them to the cover of the sparse trees. Only to be surprised to find that another group of people were already there.

A large pavilion of bright red-and-green waxed cloth was pitched in the grove, providing a decent amount of shelter from the rain. At the center of the pavilion, seated on a wooden stool, was a Losanti woman of approximately middle age, her black hair starting to reveal streaks of gray. She was dressed in brightly colored cotton wraps, which accented her mahogany colored skin. Surrounding her was a cadre of four men, all of them garbed in only a white cotton kilt. Their bullhide shields and long spears were neatly stacked nearby and one of the men walked towards the weapons as Silas and Waif approached.

Silas stopped a distance away and gestured for Waif to join him. Silas rummaged around in his saddlebags and brought out a silver talisman in the shape of a small fish, which he tied around Waif's wrist. "This should overcome any language barrier between you and the Losanti. All you have to do is speak normally and they'll be able to understand you, and you them."

"What about you?" Waif asked.

"I have a smattering of their language, I should be able to get the general gist of what they're saying. But this woman is traveling with a warrior escort, either her husbands or her sons, and at her age, quite frankly, it could be either. In either case, she's important and wealthy enough to support four dedicated warriors so it would be *grossly* improper for me to speak to her directly. Think of her as, well, sort of like Lady Gavreau."

Waif nodded and tried to not let their nervousness show. They approached the woman and at a respectful distance away stopped and bowed. "Honored mother, my father and I humbly ask permission to share your shelter as we were caught unaware in the rains." The pendant translated Waif's words seamlessly and the Losanti men turned to their matriarch for guidance.

The woman replied to Waif, and Silas managed to catch enough to let him know they had been invited to wait out the rain beneath the pavilion as guests. When Waif turned to Silas, he stepped forward and bowed to the woman as well before taking a seat with Waif on the ground.

"She wants to know what brings us here so ill-prepared during the rainy seasons," Waif said.

"No sense in trying to hide our purpose," Silas replied. "Tell her we're looking for those who walk the Path of Pakhet and wish to enlist their aid in a quest."

Waif repeated what Silas had said and waited as the matriarch replied in her own tongue, this time too rapidly for Silas to follow. "She says that a sept of the Path of Pakhet is nearby, a little less than a day's journey to the south following this trail." Waif pointed towards the break in the grasses which was rapidly turning into mud beneath the driving rains. "She's also offering to escort us to the next village and give us the gift of hospitality since we are clearly so destitute to have to travel alone."

"Has she offered her name?"

"Imani of the village of Maji Matamu, daughter of Marjani, daughter of Mwamini."

"Please tell the honorable Imani that we will be glad to take her hospitality."

* * *

The rain had continued for the rest of that day and well into the night. Silas was worried that they would end up getting flooded out by the torrents of water, but the space under the trees somehow did not become a flooded morass. The clouds cleared briefly at dawn and despite the rains, the road to the south was passable. Imani had her four sons, for it turned out the young men with her were in fact her adult sons, take down the pavilion and pack their possessions in rucksacks. In return for Imani's hospitality, Silas offered use of their horses to help carry the load, which earned him some amount of favor with Imani's sons.

As they began following the road south, Imani's sons began to sing with great enthusiasm. Silas caught only parts of the song, which was ostensibly about great deeds in battle and how they would impress the women at home, but some of the song seemed to be idioms which made absolutely no sense. Silas had Waif ask Imani about it and her response was, "The singing helps keep the predators away. Lions and manticores will avoid humans if they can, so singing gives them plenty of time to get away."

"But what if it's a man-eater and the singing only attracts it?" Silas asked.

"Well now, that's what the spears are for, aren't they?" Imani winked when she finished that sentence; Silas inferred much of her meaning before Waif had finished translating. As the day continued Silas had second thoughts about giving Waif the translation amulet as they turned redder and redder from embarrassment as the songs apparently went into subject matter most people would be hesitant to mention before their mothers. Apparently not so in Losanti. Silas merely rolled his eyes in frustration.

In the late afternoon they spotted what looked like a very large collection of stunted thorn trees but turned out to be a carefully cultivated hedge designed to keep livestock in and predators out. Between the hedge and the village proper were fields, row after row of long, dirt mounds where men dressed much like Silas walked, occasionally stopping to weed their surroundings. The fine fabrics of the men and occasional women, some of which Silas recognized as trade goods from further north, meant this community was clearly thriving.

The village itself was made mostly of rammed-earth buildings, colored in bright reds and yellows, in simple geometric designs. More men were in the village repairing the buildings under the supervision of the women. Children played in the streets, racing grass boats in puddles or kicking around an inflated cow's bladder in an ad hoc game. A woman, dressed in a bright red kitenge patterned with yellow flowers, stepped from one of the buildings and approached their party. A rapid exchange between her and Imani proceeded in the Losanti language, too fast for Silas to follow, and even Waif seemed to be having trouble keeping up.

"I think she's sort of like the mayor of this village?" Waif said, whispering to Silas as Imani and the woman continued to converse. "They spent a long time saying their names and then their mothers and then their grandmothers, and then their great-grandmothers."

"That's an old tradition, something we don't do anymore in the lands of the Empire," Silas explained. "They're trying to establish a common ancestry or traditional ties of friendship. Something that ties them together." Silas caught the Losanti word for foreigner and saw Imani gesturing towards Waif, him, and Bundersnoot. "What are they saying now?"

"Imani's just saying she met us on the road and we wanted to meet those Path of Pakhet people." Imani beckoned Waif over, and they looked back towards Silas for clarification.

"Just answer any questions the best you can. Tell the truth. Well, most of the truth."

"Okay, dad," Waif said sarcastically and walked over to join the two women.

"How's the kid holding up?" Bundersnoot asked from his perch on Waif's saddle, eyeing the soggy ground suspiciously. "And why do you keep taking me places that are wet?"

"Waif is doing fine. I hope. And we're just here during the rainy season, you should see this place during the dry season."

"Why couldn't we have come here then?"

"Because the dry season isn't for another four months and this is something I'd rather not procrastinate on."

"How's your arm?" Bundersnoot asked, unable to see for himself because of Silas's own concealing robes of black.

"The lunar caustic has been helping a lot. The wound is still there but it doesn't seem to be spreading for now. I don't know how long it will keep working, though."

"I've noticed you've been taking your meat rarer than you usually do." Bundersnoot said.

"I just wanted to try something different," Silas protested.

"Different? Silas, the meat you had at the fort was practically still mooing when you ate it! I'm worried you're going to pounce on some small furry creature and start ripping it apart with your teeth."

Silas had to take a moment as he suppressed the mental image; a part of him took perverse pleasure in the idea. It was only a gentle nip from Bundersnoot that brought him back to reality. "Everything's starting to taste so dry," Silas explained. "I'm having trouble eating the jerky and the waybread. Pottage is better but I keep finding it lacking something. It's only when I eat rare meat that I feel satisfied."

"Sounds like the curse is getting worse," Bundersnoot said, looking up at his friend with concern. "Are your dreams back too?"

"Sometimes. They're not as intense as they used to be. I had rather hoped..." whatever thought Silas had was derailed when he saw Waif waving them over. "Ah, I think they've decided they want us now." He approached with the horses behind him, bowing to the woman in the red and yellow kitenge.

"This woman is Amani, daughter of Julisha, daughter of Nyimbo and she is the headwoman of this village. She said she will take us to the sept and make introductions, but she makes no promises whether they will eventually help us or not."

Silas bowed again to Amani. "Please offer her our thanks and say we are ready to meet with the sept at any time that is convenient to her." Silas waited as Waif translated and Amani merely offered a curt response and began walking through the village. Lacking any other directions, they had no choice but to follow.

In the center of the village was one building decorated differently from the others. This building had not been painted so the walls retained the natural russet brown of the region's earth. Proudly displayed on the walls were the pelts of many animals: lions, hippopotamuses, manticores, and even the hide of one savanna dragon were prominently displayed. Each one was a testament to the skill of the hunters who had slain these dangerous predators. Two women, garbed only in white cotton kilts and holding spears just like those carried by Imani's sons, guarded the building's entrance.

Silas hitched the horses to a convenient post as Amani spoke with the guards, who did not seem happy about Amani's words but grudgingly stood aside. Silas removed one of the saddlebags and Bundersnoot jumped onto Silas's shoulder as they all entered the building. The walls themselves were several feet thick, providing a cool environment much more comfortable than the humid exterior, and set with the high lattice windows that allowed a surprising amount of light into the interior. The chamber they entered had several women seated on low stools, all of them clearly well past sixty, with gray hair and the wrinkled skin of old age. But all of their eyes were bright and looked at Silas and Waif with suspicion.

Amani made a series of ritual greetings to the assembled elders and began making introductions. Once the proper forms were satisfied, Amani shepherded Waif forward and told them to address the elders. Waif looked back towards Silas with a plaintive "What do I do?" look on their face. "Just give them a little background and tell them why we're here," Silas said encouragingly. "I'm sure you can do it."

Waif took a deep breath and then turned to face the women. "My father and I have traveled many days and many miles to request your aid. In order to work a great magic, my father requires the stinger of a manticore but he is no hunter. So we have come to you, the followers of the Path of Pakhet, to enlist your aid." The women seemed satisfied with Waif's explanation and turned to speak amongst themselves.

"Good work, kid." Silas gave Waif an encouraging pat on the shoulder. "Where did you find all the flowery language?"

"I just thought to myself how you would talk if you were trying to get more money out of Lady Gavreau or somebody else on the Council." Silas heard a laugh from his shoulder but when he looked, Bundersnoot was merely yawning innocently. Silas reflected on how far Waif had come from that scared, disheveled, catatonic child he and Bundersnoot had rescued that past summer. Waif would be forever changed by that experience, as would anyone, but Silas could see how those wounds were starting to heal. He was confident with time Waif would grow into a confident, well-grounded adult. If only he could get more time to make sure that happened.

Silas's thoughts were interrupted by the elders finally making a decision. "We shall permit you the services of one of our *winda*, as well as many porters as may be needed. However, because you are strangers to us and because of the danger of this task, we shall require your payment in advance."

Silas opened his saddlebag and withdrew a roll of cloth. He carefully placed it on the floor in front of the women and unrolled it, revealing several small objects. None of them were crafted from precious materials but even someone unattenuated to the powers of magic could sense a fragment of the raw power contained within them. Silas reached towards the first item, a bronze cylinder about a foot long and an inch in diameter. "Through careful study of ancient magics, I have managed to recreate a motionless rod." Silas picked the cylinder up and held it in the air before the women. He clicked a button set into one end of cylinder and removed his hand. The rod remained suspended in midair, in complete defiance of gravity. "The button allows the rod to remain fixed in place and it can only be moved with great difficulty. Unless, of course..." Silas pressed the button again and the rod fell, landing on the cloth below. Silas waited as Waif translated his brief speech to the council. Whether the elders were impressed with this offering or not their faces remained blank so Silas went to the next object.

He picked up three arrows, each one made from rowan wood, tipped with a flint arrowhead that had been knapped to a razor-sharp point. They were fletched with feathers from ravens that Silas had captured at a crossroads where a murderer had been hanged. "By themselves, these arrows will penetrate almost any magical barrier. Inscribed with the true name of a mage, even the most inexperienced archer will find the enemy's heart." Silas carefully put the arrows back down, as if they might jump up and pierce him at any moment.

Finally Silas picked up a silver bell, polished to a mirror shine and inscribed with runes of power. He was very careful to ensure that it did not chime while he handled it. "This bell can drive out even the most powerful of incorporeal spirits. You may attempt to bind a spirit with its power but it shall be limited and require constant vigilance."

The women consulted as Silas carefully wrapped his offerings back into the bundle. Waif strained to hear what they were saying but either a limitation of the translation charm or some defensive magic of their own left Waif as clueless as Silas. After very little consultation, the elders turned back to Waif and Silas and spoke with one voice. "Your offerings to the sept are acceptable. Return here tomorrow and you shall meet

ACROSS AMASTICA

your *winda*." The audience completed, Silas and Waif bowed and exited the chamber, following Amani's example.

* * *

"No! You can't make me go out when it's nice and safe in here!" Bundersnoot was perched on a shelf inside a guest room of Amani's own house and he hissed whenever Waif or Silas tried to get near to him. The morning was unpleasantly wet, with rain coming down in buckets, and Bundersnoot was having none of this going outside nonsense.

"Bundersnoot, we need to go. We told the Sept of Pakhet we would meet them." Silas tried to reach for Bundersnoot and was met with a swipe of claws which he narrowly dodged.

"What's this 'we' nonsense? *You* have to go out in the rain and the mud and the unpleasantness to get a Manticore stinger. *I* don't need to go *anywhere*."

"Can you try the catnip again?" Waif asked.

"You wouldn't dare!" Bundersnoot protested.

"I can't, the bag it was in leaked so it got all moldy," Silas said. "It's only good for a short period of time anyway. All right, Waif, he's made his point. He's not coming with us so let's go meet our *winda*. I hope you have a plan for food, Bundersnoot."

Bundersnoot's eyes narrowed in suspicion. "Just what exactly are you implying, Silas?"

"Hm?" Silas stopped at the door and looked back. "Oh, I just noticed that around here, cats largely work for their meals. Hunting mice, small birds, that sort of thing. You didn't happen to pick up Losanti while I wasn't looking, did you?"

"You know damn well that I didn't." Bundersnoot paced nervously on the shelf and then finally deigned to jump down.

"All right, you win this round, wizard."

"Come on, we're going to be late if we dilly-dally any longer," Waif said.

Fortunately it was a very short walk from Amani's home to the building owned by the village's sept. There were already multiple male porters, dressed only in simple cotton kilts and waxed rain cloaks, lined up outside with baskets of provisions. One of the elderly women who formed the council was standing outside, speaking with a woman with a massive crossbow strapped to her back. Waif and Silas bowed respectfully as they made their approach.

"Greetings, travelers, we have found a *winda* who speaks your language." The elder pointed towards their winda. She was a tall woman, thin but with a sinewy, whipcord strength beneath her ochre-brown skin. Her black hair was carefully woven into an intricate braid to keep it safely out of the way. She was dressed in yellow-green cotton trousers and shirt, the colors not quite matching between the two pieces but would make her difficult to spot on the savanna. The crossbow she carried was a work of exquisite craftsmanship, the wood and bronze lovingly polished and maintained, and a leather quiver of bolts hung at her waist.

"I am Barika, daughter of Siti, daughter of Nala," Barika said in mostly-correct Amastican. "My mothers have walked the Path of Pakhet for generations. I have three pelts worthy of display upon the sept's walls to my name." She gestured towards the male porters who were gathering supplies. "These are my brothers, they have followed me on many hunts and I can vouch for all of them. My eldest brother, Zakia, is my spear carrier and their leader. If you have any issues you bring them to me or Zakia."

ACROSS AMASTICA

Silas stepped forward and whispered in Waif's ear. "Understood, Mistress Barika, we shall follow your direction in all things. Have you hunted a manticore before?"

"Once. I pursued my quarry for three days and nights, thinking that I could drive it to ground. Unfortunately it escaped my clutches at the last." Barika's face hardened, clearly displeased to admit failure even against a creature as intelligent and dangerous as a manticore. "However, I know where that particular creature makes its den, three days from here. It will be less active during the rainy season so I have every reason to believe we shall be successful."

"Lead, Mistress Barika, and we shall follow."

Barika gave some orders in Losanti to her brothers, six in total, and they lifted their baskets of supplies. Which one was Zakia was made obvious because of the bundle of bronze-tipped spears he carried over one shoulder. Barika led the column out of the village towards the yam fields, Silas and Waif following on their horses at the rear of the line.

It drizzled throughout the day and Bundersnoot complained immensely to anybody who would listen, but when Silas suggested he could head back on foot, Bundersnoot briefly stopped. Towards nightfall they established a camp in a grove of acacia trees, using a series of heavy tarps to help keep the rain off. Barika's brothers got to the business of making a fire and getting the evening meal ready while Barika supervised. Taking advantage of the remaining light, Silas sat down with Waif and removed a bestiary from his pack.

"All right, Waif, let's see how your reading's coming along." Silas sat down and opened the book under the protection of their shelter. Waif joined him and started reading aloud.

"The manticore is a ferocious predator and eats only the

flesh of human beings. Its body has the head of a human, the body of a lion, the tail of a scorpion, and the wings of a bat. It is native to the plains of Losanti and the people there live in constant fear of the manticore. It is said that a child does not receive a name until the age of ten because so many of their children are eaten by manticores."

Waif paused their reading when a delighted chuckle interrupted. They looked up to see Barika laughing. "Is that what you really think about manticores? Gods above, no wonder you needed to come to us for help." Barika sat down and joined them, looking at the illustrations in the bestiary. "No, I've never seen one with wings. I don't know how that silly myth got started. And they eat plenty of things that aren't people, if they didn't, they'd probably all be dead of starvation by now."

"Well, I suppose I should have been suspicious of this book when the author started mentioning giant ants that mine gold," Silas grumbled.

"Oh, those exist," Barika said. "I've seen them with my own two eyes. You don't see them this far north, though; they're further south in the Nebian Desert." Barika traced the illustration of a manticore with her finger, examining the brushwork some unnamed scribe had put hours of effort into over a hundred years ago. "It's remarkably accurate, minus the wings and the head. Their heads are more lion-shaped and covered in fur. But their eyes, you can tell there's a cunning intelligence there. I saw it the first time I hunted a manticore and it scared me stiff. If my mother hadn't been with me I would have died that very day."

"Have you been hunting long?" Waif asked.

"Since I was your age, or perhaps a little earlier. My mother was so proud when she bore me, finally a daughter to continue the family tradition." Barika unslung her crossbow and took a leather wallet from her belt, which, when opened, revealed a collection of fine tools and bottles of oils. Barika started inspecting her crossbow, occasionally applying oil as needed to mechanisms. "When I finally came of age, she gave me this crossbow and told me it would be my most important companion. Some day my brothers might marry off and have to join their wives' households but my crossbow would be my companion for life." She paused, making extremely fine adjustments to the crossbow, and then gave the string a flick. It twanged and she seemed satisfied with the result so she began to put her tools back. "Although I worry that my homeland no longer offers me challenges."

"You mean a manticore isn't dangerous enough for you?" Bundersnoot asked. "I didn't realize the people of Losanti were so casual in their relationship with mortal peril." Silas tried to shush the cat but Barika just laughed.

"Not all Losanti, no, but very true for myself. I have long experience with the dangers of the savanna and I begin to feel my skill fading from familiarity. Eventually, I will make a simple mistake that will prove deadly. I need new challenges, different places to hunt, novel dangers that will make me feel caution again. That's why I learned your language, I hope to go north once this hunt is completed and I have conquered the greatest predator of Losanti."

"Well if we all manage to survive, we would gladly take you as far north as Elade-voc if you want," Silas said. "Although I don't know how many dangers there will be for someone used to tracking lions and manticores."

"I shall find them," Barika said confidently. "A hunter shall always find quarry wherever you send her and I thank you for your offer. However, we have an early day tomorrow. I recommend that we get as much sleep as we can. I bid you goodnight." Barika bowed to Waif and gave a curt nod to Silas, before rejoining her brothers.

"Come on, Waif," Bundersnoot said as he kneaded out a spot in Waif's bedroll for him to sleep. "You can give me a treat before we go to bed."

"Bundersnoot!" Silas cried in exasperation. "If you keep sneaking treats, we won't have enough food to get home! And then what will you do? Hmm?"

"I'm confident the gods will provide." Bundersnoot closed his eyes and it was clear he considered this conversation closed.

Silas sighed and climbed into his own bedroll. "Goodnight, Waif. Don't let him eat up all your rations when you're not looking. Otherwise, we may have to eat him." Bundersnoot pointedly ignored this jab.

"Goodnight, Silas," was Waif's only response.

* * *

The next day passed uneventfully, despite the strong showers of rain which made their progress slow, the trails turning to mud beneath them and forcing the whole party to walk through patches of tall grass to make any progress at all. Barika seemed confident they would reach the manticore's den sometime tomorrow, with plenty of daylight left to at least make a reconnaissance of the ground.

But it was sometime in the depths of that night that Silas awoke to the sounds of screaming as Bundersnoot desperately tried to wake up Waif. "Silas, I need help!" Bundersnoot cried as he took another punch from a sleep-fighting Waif. "They're having a nightmare again and I'm struggling to keep their emotions from overloading!"

"Well, what do you want me to do?" Silas asked. "Do you need me to be a reservoir again?"

"No, I just need you to keep them from flailing around!" Bundersnoot yowled as another fist connected with his stomach. "I can't do anything if they keep fighting me like this!"

Silas grabbed both of Waif's arms and pinned them to their sides, wrapping Waif in a bear hug as Waif tried to wriggle free. "By the Empress, they're slicker than a greased pig."

"Just hold onto them a little longer," Bundersnoot said as he focused his magic into helping Waif calm down. Gradually, Waif stopped fighting against Silas and their eyes opened, unfocused with the delirium of sudden wakefulness. Silas released his hold on Waif and they stretched.

"What happened?" Waif asked, rubbing sleep from their eyes. "Wait, I remember now. I had a nightmare again, didn't I?"

"Just a little stronger than usual," Bundersnoot said, looking up from Waif's lap. "Silas was extremely worried but I knew it would work out in the end." Silas rolled his eyes but he let the lie pass. He was too tired to argue with Bundersnoot at this time of night.

Waif pet Bundersnoot in silence for a few moments, avoiding eye contact with either of them, before finally looking at Silas. "Would it be okay if I got a hug? I would feel a lot better and a little safer."

"Of course you can ask for a hug, Waif." Silas scooted over and wrapped Waif again in a slightly less fierce bear hug. Silas had learned how to bear hug from the best of them. His old adventuring party member Gerald, a friend of old Narses's family, had been an accomplished swordsman and duelist but also a romantic poet and notorious flirt. His tremendous strength could be employed with remarkable gentleness to make anyone feel safe and comforted. Though Gerald could just as easily make it feel like your bones were in danger of being crushed.

Bundersnoot purred as they all sat together in companionable silence. After several minutes Silas said, "There's nothing wrong with you, Waif. You went through hell and all of us are lucky to be alive after that incident. Maybe the pain will heal with time, maybe it won't. It's too early to say. However Bundersnoot and I will be here for you every step of the way. You can count on that."

Waif looked up at Silas, rubbing the tears from their eyes. "Thank you, Silas." They picked up Bundersnoot and gave him a kiss on the head. "Thank you, Bundersnoot. You're both wonderful people." Silas let Waif go and they settled down in their bedroll. In mere moments Waif was once again in a deep, peaceful slumber.

"Not to ruin a touching emotional moment," Bundersnoot said, his green eyes boring into Silas, "but if we don't take care of this curse you may not be around much longer for Waif. And that's *if* the cure works at all."

Silas rubbed his arm over the corrupted wound, all too aware of how many caveats were attached to this plan. Even assuming they got the manticore stinger, there was still the challenge of finding a unicorn – a *true* unicorn – and those had been vanishingly rare a century ago. "Bundersnoot, if this doesn't work out and I have to…take care of the problem… I want you to stay with Waif."

"Of course I'm going to stay with Waif," Bundersnoot sniffed. "They feed me better than you do."

Silas groaned in exasperation. "Bundersnoot, I'm trying to be serious."

"Food is serious business!"

Silas bopped the cat on his head and Bundersnoot gave a small yowl of surprise. "You know perfectly well what I mean. If this cure doesn't work out and I die, I need you to take care of Waif. At least until Lady Gavreau digs up their parents or she just adopts Waif herself."

"All right, I think I can do that." Bundersnoot licked his paws for a moment, thinking. "Do you really think she'll find them?"

"I don't know. When I was confident Waif had the basics of scrying down I asked them if they'd like to find their parents. They didn't seem too keen on the idea so I didn't press the issue. I'm wondering if maybe I should have."

"Now that you mention it, there's something that bothers me about this whole situation."

"What's that?"

"It's been what, a good four, five months since we rescued Waif? In all that time I haven't heard anything about people looking for a missing child matching Waif's description. If their parents were looking, surely we'd have heard *something* by now."

Silas frowned, unsettled by the implications. "Wouldn't be the first time parents handed a mouth to feed over for a little coin and didn't ask too many questions."

"Could try asking Waif again about what happened. They might trust you enough to talk."

Silas looked at the sleeping child. Asleep, they looked even younger and more fragile than Silas knew they were. Waif had been sorely tested but that had revealed a hidden strength. Properly nurtured, Silas had no doubt they could accomplish great things in the future, but they would need a safe environment to grow first.

"Well I'm going back to sleep, you can spend the rest of the night fretting if you want but I wouldn't recommend it. We've got a manticore to hunt tomorrow." Bundersnoot walked over to Waif and found a spot on their chest that seemed comfiest and settled into a loaf before closing his eyes.

Silas climbed into his own bedroll listening to the rain patter off the canvas roof of their shelter. "Good night, Bundersnoot." An indelicate cat snore was the only response he got.

* * *

The rain was pouring down in buckets that day, so heavy it was hard for anyone to see more than a few feet in front of them. "This is good weather for hunting," Barika said as she wrapped a waterproof cloak around herself. Only she, Silas, and Zakia were going out to the manticore's den. "The manticore will stay in its den today, it will not hunt in rain like this. If we are very lucky, we may come upon it sleeping." She checked her crossbow and seemed satisfied with its condition.

Silas turned to Bundersnoot, who was perched on top of a basket desperately trying to avoid the puddles that managed to leak under the cover of their shelter. "Silas, why in the name of the Empress did we come here during the rainy season? I hate this."

"No choice, old friend. You watch out for Waif."

"Yes, Silas."

"If I don't make it back, do you remember where the money's hidden?"

"Yes, Silas."

ACROSS AMASTICA

"And the extra key to get back into the shop."

"Buried in the window box because every plant you touch dies and you're stalling! You go hunt a manticore and you better come back. If you don't, I'm going to be very upset with you."

Silas crouched down and rubbed Bundersnoot's head affectionately. "I know, if I don't come back you'll waste away to nothing because nobody will feed you."

"Well, there's hope of training Waif properly yet. Go on you, scoot."

Silas fastened his rain cloak and joined Barika and Zakia. "So, master powerful wizard, what great magics are within your powers to aid us in this hunt?" Barika asked, taking the lead and expecting Silas to follow. "What elements can you conjure? What shades do you have under your command?"

"Fire and lightning if you need it." Silas looked up at the rain pouring down ensuring anything not covered was becoming thoroughly wet. "Although I think lightning would probably be easier to do right now than fire. I'm rather good at illusions if you want to make use of those. I'm afraid anything big would take several hours to set up."

"Those may be good enough. We have hunted manticores without magic before. I shall have to see the lay of the land before I know. But best to know every arrow that's in your quiver before you need to use it."

They marched through the rain for hours, following tracks that only Barika, and perhaps Zakia, recognized. The red-orange mud clung to Silas's boots and made a thick film, forcing him to stop every half hour or so to scrape the mud off with some grass or a rock. The Losanti, wearing rugged leather sandals, seemed unaffected by the splatters of brightly

94

colored mud by dint of long experience. Eventually Barika raised one arm bringing the two men to a stop.

She pointed towards a copse of baobab trees about half a mile away, with several dead trees piled in a rough lean-to shape around the base of one tree. "That may be our manticore den," she said. "The only things on the savanna that make shelters like that are humans and manticores. We'll approach from downwind and see if we can get closer. Are you able to mask our scent with your magic?"

"Possibly, I haven't tried before," Silas admitted.

"The only reason the manticore hasn't caught our scent yet is the rain is drowning most of the smells. Using the wind will help us, but we can't rely on that alone."

Silas thought about what the savanna smelled like in his mind. The rich scent of the earth, part clay and part soil. The sweet scent of the grasses as they rustled in the breezes. The important smell of water, or at least the presence of it which was omnipresent now and so important in the dry season. And the hundreds of plant and animal smells that made up the background of the savanna.

Silas carefully wove the illusion around them, different than his usual magics designed to confuse senses of sight and sound. It was difficult at first, figuring out a new way to utilize his magic, but rapidly became easier once he thought about what he needed. He took trace elements from the land all around them, the energy of the savanna itself, and nudged it into a dome that encompassed all of them. Carefully, he also wove in a minor shielding spell which would hopefully keep their own scent from diffusing. It felt good to stretch his brain and use familiar magic in new and interesting ways.

"All right, I think I've done it." Silas said, opening his eyes.

Aside from a half-seen shimmer in the air there was no other sign to indicate that any magic had taken place. But anyone standing within the dome felt in their bones the thrum of background magic.

"Most impressive, master wizard. This should aid us greatly." Barika started her advance again, taking care to break up her walking so the regular sound of footsteps did not give them away. Slowly, carefully, they inched closer to the lean-to. About five hundred feet away, Barika called for another halt and gestured for Silas to join her. "Can you smell that?" she asked Silas in a whisper, and he sniffed the air.

"Smells like a very wet cat with just a hint of rotten meat," he said at last.

"Manticores like to cache food during the rainy season so they don't have to hunt as frequently. It will start to go bad but that doesn't seem to bother the manticore any," Barika explained. "It means we've definitely found a manticore's den and there's a very good chance they're at home as well."

Their earlier progress, slow as it had been, seemed like a full-tilt run compared to the glacial pace Barika adopted. Silas did not know how much time they made completing that final distance to the den but it felt like an eternity. As they finally came up to the wall of the lean-to, Barika made a series of hand gestures which Zakia understood, because he separated from the two of them and began climbing one of the baobab trees. Barika leaned over and spoke directly in Silas's ear. "Do you have a spell that can give me light?"

"Of course, a very simple spell."

"I need to be able to see into the den but we don't want to spook the manticore." Barika pointed to a gap in the shelter's wall. Silas put one eye up to the hole and immediately understood what Barika meant. He could make out a number of shapes, any one of which could be the manticore they sought, but without better light from the sun they remained indistinct. Silas looked up at the lean-to. It reminded him of a beaver dam he had seen once further north. Branches were arranged in a haphazard manner to form a shelter, which kept the interior mostly dry, but there were plenty of holes which allowed light in.

"I think I have an idea," Silas said, keeping his voice barely audible. Summoning light was one of the first spells most wizards learned. Even a total neophyte such as Waif could light up the darkest dungeon with a little practice. But manipulating that light, getting it to do what you wanted, took the training of a true master. Silas channeled the magical energies and crafted a small sphere of light in the air above them, carefully calibrating its brightness so the light it gave off seemed just like sunshine peeking in through a break in the clouds. By gradually increasing the light's intensity, he made it seem perfectly natural. Silas smiled, impressed by his own ability.

If Barika was impressed she made no comment, instead turning her attention to the manticore's den. It seemed Silas's efforts had been enough because she took her crossbow and aimed it through a gap in the wall. Barika held her breath, steadying her aim, and gently squeezed the crossbow's trigger. There was a twang as the string released, followed by a roar from within the den. Barika was already levering the string of her crossbow, years of training and cool professionalism making her movements swift and precise. In no time at all she had her weapon reloaded and ready to fire. She moved to another spot along the shelter wall and fired, barely stopping to aim this time. But it seemed her bolt flew true as they heard another angry roar.

The enraged manticore bounded out of its den, ready to fight whatever creatures had dared to interrupt its slumber. It paused, unleashing a mighty roar which simultaneously expressed its anger, its frustration, and its determination to murder whatever had decided today was the day. The face was disturbingly human, lacking any fur whatsoever and revealing the manticore's light brown skin underneath. The amber-colored eyes seemed able to analyze your every weakness and utilize them against you to deadly effect. The rest of its body, excluding the chitinous tail, was nearly twelve feet long and covered in tawny brown fur, clearly leonine but built on a larger, more powerful scale.

Any one of these would have been bad enough, but it was the tail which frightened Silas the most. Made of segments of dark brown chitin, the tail alone added another six feet to its already enormous size. At the end of the tail was an onyx-black stinger, long enough to pierce straight into a human's heart; a drop of the milky-white venom beading on the tip would kill him in a second. Silas was rooted to the spot, too terrified to move, as the manticore tensed its muscles to pounce. Before it could leap a bronze spear plunged into the manticore from above, piercing its hide and hopefully hitting something important.

The manticore howled in pain and whirled, scratching at the baobab tree's trunk and climbing towards Zakia. Zakia threw another spear, this one less accurate, as it bounced off the manticore's shoulder and only further enraged the beast. Zakia climbed further into the branches of the tree, nimbly keeping well out of reach of the manticore's massive paws as it redoubled its efforts. This distraction had bought Barika enough time to reload her crossbow and prick the beast with a third dart. The manticore seemed so shocked at this affront that it slid back down the tree, landing on the ground in a disorganized heap.

"We've got it now," Barika said, holstering her crossbow and drawing a curved dagger from her belt. "Entering the final part of the dance."

She advanced slowly towards the manticore, the dagger in a low guard position with her other arm extended for balance. The manticore managed to stand up and shook its head, but its hesitant steps towards Barika were groggy, as if it was having trouble controlling its movements. It launched its tail towards Barika, who dodged and struck with her dagger, scoring a deep gash on its flesh, before jumping back out of its reach. The manticore legs seemed to falter and it ended up tripping over its own feet. As it did, Barika dashed in, mounting the manticore's back and grabbing its mane. She plunged her dagger into the monster's exposed throat, cutting a long slit that severed both jugular veins, hot, red blood spurting onto the grass.

With her back turned, she did not see the manticore's tail make a final strike as the body died. Whether a final conscious thought or simple reflex, the tail moved unerringly towards Barika.

"Barika, look out!"

Silas reacted without thought, summoning magic to create a disc of energy and light, no more than a foot in diameter. The stinger bounced off the shield, deflected enough to land harmlessly next to rather than inside of Barika. Barika herself looked shaken, acutely conscious that her indiscretion in the moment of triumph could have proved fatal.

Silas approached cautiously, keeping the shield active in case there were any last strikes from the manticore. It seemed that the manticore's spirit had gone with its life blood, and after a few minutes, it was clear the creature was truly dead. Barika looked up at Silas. "Thank you, wizard, your quick thinking saved me."

"Experience working with adventurers," Silas offered by way of explanation. "Sometimes a party member doesn't notice a danger and you step in to help. That's how you survive. Incidentally, what did you drug the manticore with?"

"A combination of poisons from various sources: poppies, hispids, crushed beetles. The compound is expensive but, I think, well worth the investment. Despite being immune to its own venom, the manticore can still be poisoned."

Silas walked over to the manticore's tail and nudged it with his staff. "I just realized I didn't think to ask this, how do we take the stinger with us?"

"Very carefully." Barika said something in the Losanti language and Zakia climbed down from his hiding place in the tree. He brought out a roll of thick leather and unrolled it on the ground. Together they placed the stinger on the leather, careful to avoid touching it directly. "The venom is extremely potent," Barika explained. "Even contact with unprotected skin can do great harm to a person. I saw a man who was paralyzed for life when he stepped on a manticore stinger in the market." Barika carefully severed the stinger from the tail with her dagger and then wrapped the stinger in the leather, cinching it tight with leather cords.

Silas lifted the parcel gingerly, making sure to keep it level to discourage any venom from leaking out. "Thank you, Barika, your aid has been absolutely vital in the completion of my quest."

"In all fairness, I would have died without your aid. All my future victories will be because of you, and for that you have my thanks." Barika clutched her hand to her heart and gave a courteous half-bow to Silas. "How are you at skinning a cat?"

Silas smiled. "If Bundersnoot were here, he would have a great many things to say about that question, most of them rather unkind. But more honestly, I'm afraid I'd make a mess of it. With a spell or two I can keep the flies away, though."

"That, Zakia will definitely appreciate. Very well, stay close. It's dangerous to wander off alone on the savanna." She said something in Losanti to her brother and they began the grisly business of claiming the manticore's pelt.

* * *

It was very late in the afternoon when they arrived back at the camp. Waif practically ran into Silas's arms with their relief seeing him return. Bundersnoot's greeting was, in typical cat fashion, far cooler. "Well, I see you've managed not to get yourself killed," Bundersnoot said, acting as if he hadn't been dreadfully worried about that very outcome. "Did we get what we came for?"

Silas lifted the bundled stinger and showed it to Bundersnoot. "I saw Barika cut it directly from the manticore myself. We could probably kill the Empress herself with it. Or at least make her seriously ill."

"So where do we head to now?" Waif asked. "We have to find a unicorn, right?"

"We do. And there's really only one place I think we've even got a chance to find one. We're going to have to go back to where the Empress first appeared from the Land of the Fae.

We have to go to Tevioch."

Coursuperieur

"The first unicorns arrived with the Empress Allie and her armies of elf warriors at the founding of the Magocracy. They were reserved as mounts for high-ranking officers and the Empress's own bodyguard. It is unknown whether the wild unicorns which inhabit the lands around Tevioch escaped from the Empress's armies or arrived through the many portals connected to the Land of the Fae. Solitary and reclusive by nature, it is unknown how many unicorns inhabit our world since the closing of the portals. However regular sightings in the lands around Tevioch suggest a viable population still lives in its en-en-environs." Waif looked up from the bestiary to Silas, puzzled by the new word. "What does environs mean?"

"It's just a fancy word for saying 'the area around a place'," Silas explained. "Writers like to have different ways of saying the same thing so they don't have to repeat themselves all the time. You're doing really well with your reading, Waif!"

"I still say we'd have been better off going through a portal to try and find a unicorn." Bundersnoot stretched in the sunlight and looked distrustfully at the boat's leaky bottom. "I would have preferred that instead of having to cross the Braelors in a floating box."

After returning home from Losanti, it had taken only a

week for the first boats to come down the Ganorne River, confirming it had thawed enough to travel to the other side of the mountains where Coursuperieur was located. Silas had booked passage for all three of them, as well as their horses and wagon, on the first boat headed upriver. Traveling on the Ganorne was the easiest way to cross the Braelors and its strategic position on this natural highway had made both Elade-voc and Coursuperieur. In hindsight, Silas admitted he should have inquired more about the suspiciously reasonable price of passage this early into the season.

They were riding in a flatboat, little more than a wooden box unimportant enough to even have a name, that had been caulked with tarred hemp. It was one in a chain of five boats being hauled upriver by the *Maid of the Marshes*. That boat was what Silas had seen at the docks of Elade-voc, a sturdy riverboat with two magic-powered paddle-wheels—one port, one starboard—allowing it to travel up and down the Ganorne with ease. Foolishly, Silas had assumed they would join the crew and better-heeled passengers. Instead they were traveling with barrels of salted meat and bales of cotton headed for the Empire's interior.

"It was the first boat headed upriver." Silas wriggled his fingers and some of the water that had seeped through the flatboat's boards bailed itself over the side. "Besides, we'll be in Coursuperieur in a few short days and we'll be safely back on dry land. Waif, let's see how you're progressing with summoning light."

Waif closed the bestiary and jumped down from their perch on a barrel. Screwing their face up, they carefully moved their hands, trying to remember Silas's instructions. Silas watched as magical energy coalesced into a small sphere a few feet in front of Waif. The sphere began to glow, a weak orange glow like a cheap tallow candle, but glow nonetheless. Waif looked at the sphere and with a physical thrust of one arm they shoved more magical energy into the sphere. The light rapidly shifted from orange to yellow to white before the sphere exploded and magical energy scattered everywhere. Waif gave a shout of frustration and dismay.

"You're getting better," Bundersnoot said encouragingly. "Last time you barely got to yellow before you lost control."

"Yes, I think I see the problem," Silas said. "When you shift to putting more energy in your control over the matrix slips. So what we do is practice control until it becomes second nature to you. Then we can work on putting more power into your spells."

"Silas, I…" Waif paused, looking down at the boat's leaky bottom and unable to make eye contact with the wizard. "I don't think I'm cut out to be a wizard."

"But you're doing so well!" Silas said. "We only started last week and you're already trying to add power, that's amazing progress!" When Silas was a neophyte no older than Waif he had struggled for weeks to get a light spell to even flicker orange. It had taken him the better part of a year to master simple light spells, to the point his teacher had despaired of ever taking him on in the first place. But once Silas's mind had shifted to understanding magic, feeling the currents of energy that went through their world, it had been so much easier.

Waif looked up, tears of frustration streaming down their face. "But magic is just so *hard*. You make it look so easy and I can't even make a simple light spell work right. I don't think I have magical ability and eventually you're going to get fed up and get rid of me." Waif was in a full meltdown at this point, sniffling as they fought the onslaught of tears.

Silas's heart broke in two. He rushed over to Waif and embraced them in a bear hug. "Oh, Waif, I would never get rid of you. Never, never, never." Bundersnoot also came over, carefully jumping from one bale of freight to another, and began nuzzling Waif. There was an unintelligible mumble from Waif and Silas leaned back. "What was that?"

Waif took a few deep breaths, composing themselves, before repeating their question. "Why did you ask Lady Gavreau to find my parents?"

Silas frowned. There had been a letter from the Lady Mayor when they'd made their brief stop home. So far, her agents had no success. There were all manner of rookeries people could disappear into, but she was still turning over rocks in Bridgegate. "I assumed they'd be worried sick that their child had gone missing and they'd want to know they were safe." Although, Silas had to admit going the better part of a year without *any* contact from their child suggested extremely careless parents.

"They sold me," Waif said.

"What?" Silas was genuinely confused. The statement didn't make any sense. Unless.

"They sold me," Waif repeated in a flat monotone, clearly working hard to keep from breaking down again. "They said they had too many mouths to feed and it was about time I paid them back for raising me. So they sold me."

Silas knew life in Bridgegate was hardscrabble, people doing their absolute best to make ends meet. It wasn't unusual for children as young as Waif to be apprenticed to some trade to help bring some money in for the family, or at least offset the cost of raising them. But to just *sell* a child, with no regard as to what might happen to them. Silas was still interested in finding Waif's parents, but now for an entirely different reason.

"Waif, look at me." Silas looked into Waif's green eyes, seeing the pain that stretched back well before the terrifying incident with the Revelers. "You will always have a home with Bundersnoot and me for as long as you want. And we will never ask for anything in return."

"I demand treats!" Bundersnoot said, interrupting their conversation. "As your liege and landlord, I demand to be fed!"

"BUNDERSNOOT!" Silas almost screamed in aggravation. "I am *trying* to have a moment here with Waif, and all *you* can think about is your thrice-damned stomach!" But he couldn't help but smile as Waif laughed.

"I still don't think I can be a wizard," Waif said. "I don't seem to have the knack for it."

"Well that's just plain nonsense," Silas said, crossing his arms. "I'm going to tell you a little secret: anybody can be a wizard."

"But don't you have to have to be born with magic?" Waif asked. "The current empress and all her court have to be wizards, don't they?"

"People who are descended from Empress Allie's bloodline have a certain affinity for magic," Silas conceded. "Strictly speaking, we call them sorcerers because magic is so linked to their ancestry, but they make up maybe a fifth of all the wizards in Amastica. I can tell you with absolute certainty that I do not have a single drop of the Empress's blood in my veins and yet I am still a wizard. Magic doesn't discriminate on who your ancestors were or whether you're the seventh child of a seventh child. The only thing required to become a wizard is the willingness to learn."

Waif pondered this for a moment. "But if anybody could become a wizard, how come everyone *isn't?*"

"That is a more complicated socioeconomic question. Let me ask you this, could anybody become a weaver?"

"I suppose so. If you can learn to operate a loom you can probably weave."

"Exactly, and weaving I might add is a very prosperous occupation. Everyone needs clothes, after all, and there are no clothes without cloth. But why doesn't everyone become a weaver?"

"Well, I guess because if everyone spent all their time weaving we'd have nothing to eat."

"Nothing to eat!" Bundersnoot's face was a study of abject horror. "What a catastrophe! We can never allow such a thing to happen! Burn the looms, everyone shall go naked from henceforth." Silas bopped Bundersnoot on the head and the cat let out a small bleat of surprise.

"You are correct, young Waif. And there are some people who just don't like weaving. They're perfectly happy to let someone else do the weaving so they can spend their time making pottery or making rope or a hundred other trades that help make the world go around."

"So if everybody became a wizard we wouldn't have anybody to do all the farming and stuff. I guess that makes sense."

"That's part of the reason," Silas said. "The rest is that the Amastican royal family jealously guards their secrets. There are rumored to be all manner of powerful, incredible spells which they share only with members of the bloodline. But the Empire cannot run without wizards and the Empress's children cannot be everywhere, so there's a certain amount of magic they grudgingly share under their own terms. Outside of the Imperial academies it's very difficult to learn how to become a wizard, but not impossible."

Waif looked apprehensive again, terrified at the prospect of being shipped off to a distant school. "You mean I'm going to have to go to one of these academies?"

"If you want to." Silas shrugged. "I never did. I learned from the Enchantress Adelle."

Waif's eyes went as wide as saucers. "*The* Enchantress Adelle? The famous Silverbark general who never lost a battle?" Silas noted Waif had apparently been reading up on recent history as well as going through his mail.

"Yes, although a lot of good her string of victories did her in the end when the Silverbarks lost the war and went into exile. As far as I know, she's still across the sea in Oltramar." Silas paused, looking at Waif, who was absolutely gobsmacked by this revelation. "Adelle taught dozens of wizards, and is probably still teaching new wizards. She disagreed intensely with the Imperial system, thought that magic should be more available, that there were uses beyond keeping the infrastructure of empire together. I just happened to be lucky enough to be in the right place at the right time to be taught by her."

"Did you fight in the war? The last one, with the Silverbarks."

"Briefly," Silas admitted. "Narses and Gerald and Robèrta, all of us ended up picking sides in that war. Robèrta and Gerald picked the Cascades, Narses and I the Silverbarks." The elder Narses had owned significant holdings east of the Braelors and as a result was steadfastly loyal to the Silverbarks. Robèrta and Gerald, on the other hand, had grown up in the intensely political climate of Tevioch and saw opportunities for advancement in backing the Cascades. Silas would have remained neutral, but Adelle had called upon the bond between teacher and student and he hadn't had the courage to say no.

The night before Gerald and Robèrta were due to leave, the old friends had gathered at one of Narses's estates to toast the old days. But as the wine flowed, so had the recriminations and it had ended in a screaming match. Bonds which had seemed unbreakable had shattered and Silas hadn't seen or heard from either of them since. "I was only in a handful of battles. One by Coursuperieur, a couple by Orvion. They were… they were bad. Probably the worst things I've ever experienced."

"Worse than adventuring?"

"Adventuring is different in its own way. It's dangerous, but people *choose* to go adventuring. War—war catches all sorts of people who didn't ask to be there. Plus adventuring usually has much better food."

This was met with a derisive laugh from Bundersnoot. "I am wasting away to nothing and you talk about food! I see how it is." Silas waved his hand and another bucketful of water from the boat's bottom rose into the air and splashed all over Bundersnoot, who yowled with indignation. "Very well, I can see how I'm not wanted around here! I shall run away on my own and find someone who appreciates my true talents!" Bundersnoot jumped from barrel to barrel, disappearing among the freight.

"Should we be worried?" Waif asked.

"No, give him a few hours to pout and he'll come back again. Anyway, to get back to my original point, you are just as capable of being a wizard as any other person in the whole wide world. But if you'd rather be a glassblower or a saddle maker or something as sordid and disgusting as a politician, Bundersnoot and I will support you."

Waif fiddled with their hands, practicing the basic gestures every wizard needed to control the flow of magic. "You really think I could be a great wizard like you someday?"

"Absolutely, not a shred of doubt in my mind."

"Well, I guess I could keep practicing."

"That's the spirit! All right, so the important thing when you're controlling magic..."

* * *

"Silas, wake up." Silas grunted and rolled over in his blanket, ignoring the insistent prodding from Bundersnoot. "Silas, come on, you need to wake up."

Silas didn't even bother to open his eyes. "Bundersnoot, it is the middle of the night. I do not care how hungry you are I am not getting up to feed you."

"There's something magic in the water out there."

This, at least, got Silas's attention. He cracked an eye open. "What sort of something magic?"

"I don't know, Silas, that's why I said 'something' instead of telling you whatever it was."

"All I ask is a night of uninterrupted sleep but for my sins the gods continue to punish me in my dotage," Silas groaned and climbed out of his bedroll.

"You had a perfectly good night of full sleep last night. Come on, it might have left already." Bundersnoot led Silas through the maze of barrels and crates to the edge of the flatboat. They looked out across the moon-dappled waters and Bundersnoot pointed his tail at a large ripple. "That right there. I can't tell what it is, but it's giving off enough magic to make my fur stand on end."

Silas leaned against the gunwale and squinted. "Looks like an ordinary river otter to me." Silas closed his eyes and let his senses spread to feel the magical energies surrounding him. The stable strength of the mountains was an earthy brown on either side of the river, mixed with the greens of the trees and other plants awakening from their winter slumbers. Beneath him, the river thrummed a bright cobalt blue, but mixed within it was an aquamarine that did not match the river. "Well now, that's interesting indeed. Who or what are you, little friend, who is giving off so much energy?" Silas leaned further over the gunwale, trying to get a better look at the otter. The otter, seeming to notice the attention it was getting, obligingly swam closer towards the flatboat and Silas reached out a hand.

"Silas, I wouldn't do that!" Bundersnoot backed away from the boat's edge nervously. "We don't know what it's capable of."

"Bundersnoot, just because you're scared of water doesn't mean I have to be as well." Silas had turned his head back to face Bundersnoot so he wasn't watching when the otter transformed into...something. The core of the creature was clearly meant to be horse but the eyes were positioned forwards like a predator and added a subtle wrongness to the creature's appearance. Instead of hair, the creature was covered in long, thick strands of water weeds that dripped down its neck. Silas barely had time to turn his head before the creature grabbed his outstretched arm in its mouth and dove under the water, dragging Silas with it.

Silas had no time to catch his breath when the creature pulled him under. He tried struggling at first, lashing out at the creature's neck until a much harder bite on his arm made him stop. Pausing, Silas considered his situation, even as his lungs began to burn for air. With a little concentration, Silas was able to bring together disparate bubbles that flowed through the river's current and shape them together into one large bubble. He carefully moved the bubble over his head and took a deep breath. It was only a temporary solution, he knew the air would go foul quickly, but it solved the immediate problem of not drowning.

He used the time to examine the rest of the creature which had him in its grip. The head and body were very similar to horse, but a deep blue-green like freshwater ponds. Its forelimbs were long flippers that allowed the creature to apply its prodigious strength to swimming through the water and instead of hind limbs it had one powerful dolphin-like tail. A memory clicked in Silas's head, a page seen in the very bestiary that Waif had been reading earlier. "You're a kelpie," he thought. "But if you're here, then that would mean..."

As if on cue, three more otters appeared and the kelpie presented Silas to them. Their eyes bored into Silas with an intensity greater than any mundane river creature could have brought to bear. As one, the three otters nodded and the kelpie released Silas from its mouth. Unburdened, Silas shot back towards the river's surface like a cork, popping out of the water and gasping in lungfuls of fresh air. "Silas!" He could hear both Waif and Bundersnoot calling for him now. Silas began swimming across the current, keeping a steady rhythm as he headed towards their voices.

In a matter of minutes, he had swum up alongside the flatboat. "Over here!" he cried out, grabbing onto the side of the boat and refusing to let go. He tried to pull himself into the vessel but his exhaustion was too great and he slid back down, almost loosing his grip. "Waif, Bundersnoot, I'm over here. Somebody throw me a rope or something!" Silas waited and felt a coil of hempen rope smack him in the face. "Waif, is this tied down to something?"

"Uh, hold on for a minute!" There was a conversation that Silas didn't quite catch which ended in an exasperated. "Because I'm the one with hands! Or do *you* want to try tying it?"

"Waif?"

"I think we're ready!" was the only response.

"Well, surely they won't let me drown," Silas muttered to himself. Although with them you could never be entirely sure. Using both hands to grip the rope, he managed to slowly pull himself out of the water, his sodden clothes weighing him down and making his effort that much harder. After what felt like an eternity, he managed to get his center of mass over the boat's gunwale and tumbled over onto an unfortunately hard crate.

"Oh, thank gods, that knot held," Bundersnoot said. "Here I was worried it would come lose."

"I *told* you I knew what I was doing," Waif replied. "Silas, what happened? What dragged you into the river?"

Silas took a moment to gather his breath before answering. "We've got some nixie who decided they want our help."

* * *

The nix (plural nixie) is a freshwater spirit similar to their saltwater cousins the selkies, tied to the genius loci of the water which they inhabit. Like all water spirits, the nix is a shapeshifter by its very nature, so their true form is a matter of speculation. Most often the nix appears as a river otter or in a humanoid form, but they are capable of becoming large fish, a beaver, and in one recorded instance a heron. Nixie are also often aided by kelpies, another shapeshifting water creature.

Waif looked up from the bestiary. "What's a genius loci?" It was two hours past dawn and Silas was in his spare clothes, laying his soaked traveling clothes out in the sun to dry out.

"It's a- oh, how to explain. So, magical energy comes from everything around us. The river, the mountains, the trees, the land, even the very air, all of them have a latent power. Magic is the art of tapping that power and getting it to do things you want. Does that make sense?"

Waif nodded.

"Now, wherever you have magical energy, you usually have some sort of spirit that guards and nurtures that magic. When wizards are being fancy they like to call these spirits genii locorum. That's the plural of genius loci, it's from old Amastican which is a travesty of a language," Silas clarified in response to the confused look on Waif's face. "The larger the source of magic, the more powerful that spirit is."

"So are they Fae?"

"Yes and no," Silas answered, wiggling his hand back and forth. "Being creatures of magic, they're certainly tied to the Land of the Fae, but their power is firmly set in this world. So they inhabit a sort of in-between space, bridging our two worlds. Bundersnoot, did you have any luck with the boatmistress?"

Bundersnoot had reappeared in the circle Silas had hastily chalked on top of a crate, which had allowed the cat to teleport between the flatboat and the *Maid of the Marshes* towing them upriver without danger of getting wet. "She's willing to stop for an hour, said she needs to recharge the magical device powering the wheels anyway. What she *didn't* say is that she and the rest of her crew are spooked by what happened with the nixie. One of the deckhands saw the kelpie drag you under, so now they're all worried they might be next, and none of them have magic to save them."

"Well, an hour should be enough to at least find out what they want. And if not, I have a feeling our boatmistress isn't about to head off without us."

In fact, it was just around the next curve of the river that the kelpie, in its true pseudo-horse form, burst up from the river and shot a stream of water from its mouth at the *Maid*. The boat's bell began to ring in panicked alarm as it steered into the riverbank, casting down its anchor. The kelpie seemed satisfied once the boat had stopped, but shot a few more bursts of water almost playfully before disappearing again beneath the river's surface. The cables connecting the flatboats with the *Maid* went taut as they were caught in the river's current. Their flatboat bumped up against the riverbank and wedged against the roots of a tree.

"I suppose this means the nixie want their meeting now," Silas said, collecting his staff and a satchel filled with magical odds and ends that might be useful. With a grunt, he climbed over the boat's side and managed to reach land with a minimum of splashing about. He leaned back over the gunwale and picked up Bundersnoot, sparing the cat from the possibility of getting wet, as Waif followed. The kelpie surfaced nearby and playfully shot a stream of water at Silas, which he nudged aside with magic.

"Yes, yes, you have our attention now. There's no need to be rude about it. Where are your mistresses?"

"Ahoy there, master wizard! Where are you off to?" This last comment was shouted by one of the mates on the paddle boat. "There's a dangerous river creature about!"

"I know! It has business with me, but what sort I don't know yet." Silas pointed towards the kelpie, who had swum a little way downriver and then turned back, looking at them expectantly. "Tell your captain she should keep the *Maid* anchored until we get back. We should have an answer for her then."

"I'll do my best," the mate replied. "But she's got a schedule to keep and wants to get to Coursuperieur. Rumor is there's a military contract in the offing."

"We'll do the best we can. All right, all right, we're coming." This last part was directed towards the kelpie, who had started splashing impatiently. Half a mile downstream, and many stumbles and splashes along the riverbank later, the kelpie led them to a pool so deep its waters were a dark blue. As they approached the shoreline, three women's heads popped up from beneath the water. All of them had dark green hair and chestnut brown skin, the same color as the fur of a river otter. Silas couldn't tell if their eyes were gray or blue as they swum towards him, the color seeming to shift in the sunlight. The women emerged from the water all garbed in gowns of the richest ultramarine blue silk embroidered with silver wave designs. Though they were shorter than Silas, their aura of dignity and power made them seem to loom over him.

Silas bowed as he would to any woman of higher station. (With the exception of Lady Gavreau, whose arrivals at his home continued to be as informal as they were irregular.) "Honored mistresses of the waters, my name is Silas and I have answered your summons. How may I, a humble wizard, be of service to you great ladies?"

"Greetings, wizard Silas," the woman in the center of the trio said. "We apologize for any shock you may have experienced in our summons. Our kelpie tends to improvise their instructions." Silas noted that no name had been offered, not unusual in dealing with magical beings whose names could be used to bind them in the service of an unscrupulous wizard. "We ask that you intercede on our behalf with the people of Coursuperieur and demand that they halt their bronze-working in the city."

Silas bowed his head in respect. "Noble ladies, forgive me, but your request begets many questions for me. I am a wizard, yes, but I have no influence within the imperial hierarchy. I could speak with the leaders of Coursuperieur but I do not know if they would heed my words. Your words would carry far greater weight from your own mouth than through a humble proxy such as myself.

"Also," Silas continued. "I am sure you are well aware the nature of your request could be...difficult to fulfill. We require bronze for so many tools, it would be difficult for any community to forego its use entirely."

"We have already attempted to speak with the Imperial Governor of the city, a member of the Cascade family," the same nix answered, her two sisters remaining silent. "Despite our repeated petitions, she delayed us for many months, and when she finally deigned to grant us an audience, she dismissed our concerns as mere folly. We fear that those who lead the Empire no longer have proper respect for we who care for this world.

"As for your second question as to why we make this request," the nix paused and considered the three of them. "I think you are trustworthy people, it shall be easier to show you."

She beckoned for the three of them to follow while her two sisters remained by the edge of the pool. She led them to a shallow cave by the shoreline, where the waters lapped over the sandstone floor and reflected sunlight brightened the cave's interior. Resting inside, on a bed made of pine boughs, was another nix.

At a glance it was obvious that she was ill. Her hair was the muddy brown of decomposing plants rather than the vibrant green of her sisters. While her skin was the same rich brown, there were large splotches of a sickly gray color all across her body. She coughed weakly and looked at her visitors but her eyes were clouded and unfocused. She and her sister spoke in a sibilant language that was unfamiliar to Silas. After a brief conversation, the ill nix lay back on her bed and returned to a troubled sleep.

"This is our sister who lives closest to Coursuperieur," the woman who led them here explained. "The waters beneath the bronze works have become riddled with poison. Nothing, not plant, not bird, not fish, can live in those waters. As the life of those waters dies, so shall she. If the poison continues to spread, it is only a matter of time before all of us succumb. I accept that it may be too late to save our sister, but for now we can still act and try to save ourselves."

Silas's arm twinged in sympathy. Last he had measured, the length of the creeping black spot along his arm was a little over a foot in length. The lunar caustic had slowed its growth, but he was still in a race against the relentless advance of a poison nonetheless. He understood all too well the horror of watching a disaster unfold. "It is not right that humans cause such destruction with no concern for its effects. We shall aid you through whatever means we can."

ACROSS AMASTICA

* * *

The next day, they were back on the flatboat, heading up river once again. It had taken persuasion from Silas and a little extra silver to convince the boat mistress to take them back on board after the incident with the kelpie. The kelpie continued to swim alongside, occasionally making the crew duck with its jets of water, but getting up to no more serious mischief than that. Silas was sure the boat mistress would be happy to see the last of them when they finally docked at Coursuperieur. Silas still didn't understand how the waters could become poisoned so quickly from bronze-working. There were plenty of dangerous byproducts of the bronze-smelting process, certainly, but no community would be stupid enough to dump them into their own water supply.

As they grew closer to the bustling river city, Silas became far less certain of that fact. Once, when he was much younger, Silas had traveled along this very river and had been impressed by the ranks of deciduous trees that stretched up the mountain slopes. Oak, elm, maple, ash, beech – all manner of trees had grown in a vibrant forest that had existed since time immemorial. It seemed that nothing done by humans could possibly encroach on that sylvan majesty. But the sounds of axes rang through the hills and they passed one such work group on the river.

Magic-fueled machines, not all that dissimilar to the walker they had encountered in Deepwater, climbed along the slopes of the hill. Under the direction of a forewoman, the machines swung their massive bronze axes and felled even the stoutest of oaks with only a few swift blows. Once a tree collapsed, gangs of men would hack off branches and reduce the trunk

120

into manageable trunks. Other men hauled the wood down to the river and slung their cargo into waiting flatboats, tethered behind another magic paddlewheeler much like the *Maid*. As they passed by, the boat mistresses signaled to each other with the silver bells of each boat and the crews waved amicably. Silas spent more time watching men and machines clear a patch of forest in a matter of minutes that might have taken days with only hand tools.

As they passed the work crews, the forests came to an abrupt end and the hills on either side of the river were devoid of anything but stumps. Deep gullies were cut in the earth where the spring rains had eroded through the dirt, revealing the red sandstone bedrock of the Braelors. In a matter of years, Silas could see this land becoming an impassable series of ragged bluffs. New life would spread into this strange land, he was certain, but he knew the forest itself might never recover. Looking upriver, he could see plumes of black smoke rising from Coursuperieur, thick enough to dim the very sun.

"I've only seen smoke that thick once in my life," Bundersnoot said, his voice tinged with concern. "That was during the Sack of Orvion."

"I remember it," Silas said. "The city burnt for three days until the rains came. We tried everything we could, but nothing could make it stop."

Waif looked up at Silas, their eyes wide. "Has Coursuperieur been attacked?"

"No." Silas shook his head. "No, everyone's acting too normal for that to have happened. We would have run into refugees fleeing downriver, everything they owned packed into boats nearly ready to sink. This is apparently business as usual."

"Coursuperieur was an imperial fort and maybe twenty

buildings the last time we came through here," Bundersnoot said.

"I remember," Silas said. "But clearly things have changed."

Along the riverbank countless furnaces glowed as men, stripped to the waist despite the spring chill, tended the fires. There were some magical devices which helped, especially with the heaviest and most dangerous labor, and even some very mundane devices. Waterwheels powered massive hammers, which then crushed ores into fine powders, that men then shoveled into furnaces that had not yet been lit. Other men tended active furnaces, carefully monitoring the combustion of the fuel and making adjustments as needed. Finally some furnaces, still radiating heat but no longer in use, gave up lumps of the refined metals that were so crucial to civilization. And everywhere, the river lapped at heaps of black slag that had been dumped anywhere it was out of the way.

Elsewhere, women carefully measured proportions of copper and tin into crucibles to create ingots of the all-important bronze, the metal which made the business of empire possible. Men loaded the finished bronze ingots onto wagons under the watchful eyes of imperial troops, who seemed to be everywhere with their white cloaks. "It looks like the entire city has been put to the business of making bronze," Silas said. "No wonder there's so much devastation."

The *Maid* finally found an empty patch of muddy riverbank and nudged its way ashore with a creak of timbers. In a matter of moments the deckhands had thrown down the anchor and gangplanks. Passengers struggled ashore with their possessions as roustabouts started to unload cargo. Trapped in their flatboat, Silas, Waif, and Bundersnoot could do nothing but wait until enough roustabouts were free to haul their own boat in for unloading.

Silas slung a pack of essentials over his shoulder, picked Bundersnoot up, and carefully disembarked from the boat. "We've got the wagon in this boat, and the two mares in the third boat down. Can you unload them and get the team hitched up?" he asked one of the more sober-looking roustabouts.

"Sure thing, sir. You have lodgings in town yet?"

"Not yet, we need to get our bearings first." Silas gave two silver coins to the man who doffed his cap appreciatively. "Take good care of our horses and gear and there will be more where that came from. Come on, Waif."

They walked up from the landing into the town proper. Coursuperieur had been built on a circle plan in the past but the rapid expansion of the town meant buildings had been erected wherever was most convenient with little thought for future expansion. Everywhere they looked, industry continued at the same frenetic pace as the metal foundries outside town.

As they walked towards the town's center, they saw countless workshops where bronze ingots were shaped and reworked into axes, spears, swords, helmets, armor, and shields. The largest workshops were engaged in crafting parts for the massive magical Devices, an immense undertaking which required the supervision of an imperial-trained wizard during every step. "It looks like they've converted Coursuperieur into the Empire's armory," Bundersnoot said. "I can't smell anything but bronze and smoke."

"I suspect the Cascades have less firm a grip on their throne than they desire," Silas said as they stood aside for yet another squad of imperial spearmen. "That, or they're preparing for something which Lady Gavreau may want to know about."

ACROSS AMASTICA

"You mean invade Elade-voc?" Waif asked, surprised by the possibility.

Bundersnoot hissed, "Quiet, you fool. You have no idea who could be listening. Let's keep our hypotheses for when we're somewhere properly warded against observation." They continued their walk in silence, save for the busy sounds of the city around them.

Fortunately they soon found an inn with a stable and vacancies available. "I can only offer you one room," the landlady said. "We're packed to the rafters as is right now with the workers and the soldiers and everything else. Mind you, the soldiers are liable to eat me straight out of business if it weren't for the bronze workers."

"That's fine," Silas said, handing over the agreed upon price. "We're not expecting to be here long. Although it's been some time since I've been through here. I was surprised to see the changes."

"Yes, hard to believe sometimes, isn't it? Ten years ago if you'd told me I'd pick up everything and move to Coursuperieur because they needed good bronze workers, I'd have asked you where Coursuperieur was. But the money my husband and his sons made was good enough to buy us this inn. And we invested in some plots on the edge of town. Price isn't where I want it yet, but it's higher than what we paid for it."

"A wise woman indeed, your husband is lucky to have such a canny woman as his wife." The room turned out to be a garret right under the inn's gabled roof. There was no bedding or so much as a stick of furniture, but fortunately, Silas and Waif had their own bedrolls ready. Bundersnoot made a circuit of the room, sniffing at various corners, while Silas chalked out a circle on the floor with various arcane symbols.

"Nothing out of the ordinary in here," Bundersnoot said, twitching his tail. "Just a crowded inn in a city fit to burst at the seams."

Silas said a few words in Old Amastican and they all felt the tingle of magical energy on their back teeth. "That should keep anyone from spying on us, whether through mundane means or magical. All right, Bundersnoot, what did you notice?"

"They're preparing for a war. They mean to strike fast and in overwhelming numbers. It *might* be against Elade-voc, but at the same time, it might not. I didn't notice any boats that were obviously troop transports along the riverbank, did you?"

"No. A large quantity of flatboats and some paddlewheelers but those can move troops just as easily as they move freight." Silas hummed thoughtfully. "Not enough data to make a proper conclusion, just supposition at this point."

"I think Gavreau would want to know about this regardless," Bundersnoot said, twitching his whiskers. "If she hasn't already got her people up here monitoring the situation, she'll want to change that in a hurry."

"At least that part is easy. I'm worried we won't be able to help save the nixie."

"Why is that?" Waif asked.

"Well, this appears to be entirely government action." Silas sat down on the floor cross-legged, and started absentmindedly petting Bundersnoot. "If it was just one or two foundries or mines, we might be able to get the local governess to lean on the trouble-makers to make them stop. But the number of men employed, the resources devoted to this, it looks like the governess, and the vicereyne above her, and the empress-regent above both of them, are all behind this. Which means

I'll have to get more hands-on."

"And that would be treason," Bundersnoot said. Waif blanched at the possibility.

"Weeeeell, yes and no," Silas hedged. "Strictly speaking, I am not a subject of her arcane majesty so I am not capable of committing treason against her. But at the same time, many rulers do not find such legal technicalities terribly relevant when their will is thwarted. Bundersnoot, I need you to get in contact with the local cats, listen to what they're talking about."

"I can do that," Bundersnoot said. "As a matter of fact, I saw a rather cute calico a few streets back..."

"No." Silas bopped Bundersnoot on the head. "You behave yourself. Last thing I need is another sack of kittens delivered." The last time Bundersnoot had an amorous interlude, influenced by a concubus in the village of Mauvaisane, Silas had received a sack of mewling marmalade kittens about six months later along with a rather angry note. It had been hell finding good homes for all three of them while planning their trip down to Losanti. Fortunately, at least one boat mistress thought marmalade cats were especially good luck.

"Fine," Bundersnoot grumbled. "You have just one little accident and are you ever allowed to live it down?"

Silas ignored the cat's griping and turned to Waif. "How do you feel about exploring the city on your own?"

"By myself?" Waif asked, nervously looking between wizard and cat. "I mean, I guess I could. I don't know how much help I'd be."

"Trust me, Waif, sometimes a child can get somewhere that a wizard cannot. Keep your eyes open and look at *everything*, you never know what might be important. But only if you're comfortable," Silas added. "I know being in a new place can be overwhelming. If you'd rather stay in the room or stick with me..."

"No, no, I think I can explore by myself for a bit," Waif said. "I want to try anyway."

Silas smiled and reached into his satchel, bringing out a bronze dagger and a coin purse. "Keep your purse hidden, although I imagine growing up in Bridgegate you know most of the tricks pickpockets use." Waif nodded in agreement. "There should be enough to pay the roustabout at the landing and a little extra if you find a small something you like. Keep the dagger hidden and don't unsheathe it unless you mean to use it. And you better have a damn good reason to use it. Escalating a situation with violence can rapidly get out of hand." Silas winced at the memory of one or two fights from his adventuring days that could have been avoided if people had been quicker to use their minds rather than their blades.

Waif picked up the dagger carefully and looked at it. "Why give me one at all, then?"

"Because if some bloody idiot comes along and tries to sell you again, I want you to stab him where it hurts, *then* run away. A stab wound does wonders for distracting someone's concentration. Now go out and be back here by sundown!" Silas rubbed out a chalk rune and the magic circle collapsed.

"Okay, *dad*," Waif said sarcastically, getting up and heading towards the door.

"And don't forget to get our horses and wagon!" Silas said before they walked out. "I don't want to have to walk all the way to Tevioch!"

After the door closed Bundersnoot looked up at Silas with his glass green eyes. "A disinterested observer might say that you are developing a parental fondness for that child. Not that I am disinterested, mind you, I am merely thinking aloud."

"Don't you have a landlady to beg food from or something?" Silas asked.

"I do." Bundersnoot flicked his tail in indignation and walked towards the door himself. "And you have important things you should be doing as well, Silas. I am merely commenting on something that is interesting to me, personally."

Silas swore at the cat in three languages for his insolence and made his own preparations to go out.

* * *

Like the rest of Coursuperieur, the imperial fortress had undergone massive changes since Silas's last visit. Twenty years ago it had been a circular tower surrounded by a pentagon-shaped curtain wall, with enough barracks for a garrison of around two hundred soldiers. A respectable garrison, for certain, but dwarfed by Elade-voc's own city garrison of three thousand. Now that original fortress was merely the inner keep to a vast, sprawling complex that had swallowed the original village. The outer walls were only a simple wooden palisade, delineating between the military and civilian realms, but Silas could see masons already at work erecting more permanent curtain walls to protect this expanded garrison.

Plenty of craftspeople were going in and out of the gate without being stopped by the guards, so Silas felt no qualms as he approached. Silas made sure to keep his pace steady and brisk as if he had somewhere important to be. The trick to sneaking into many places was to make it look like you belonged there, a skill he had learned from his party-member, Robèrta. She had even demonstrated on one memorable occasion how, though wearing the same clothes, a person acting authoritatively could easily get into places they couldn't get by acting furtively. The two spearmen gave him only the cursory of looks as he walked straight past them, and returned to scanning the crowd for possible trouble.

Inside the palisade the busy hubbub of the city was concentrated, the sounds and smells more intense in this confined space. He had to keep moving just to keep from getting trampled in the swarm of activity. Eventually Silas was able to locate the core of the old garrison and headed in its direction, assuming that anybody who was in charge would probably be in the center. Once again, Silas's aura – which transmitted a very official, "I'm very important and I'm in a hurry" air about him – managed to get him through the gate with no trouble into the heart of the fortress.

The stone walls were unchanged, stained by rain and time but still an impressive series of fortifications that would have held off all but the most prepared attackers. Various buildings, including barracks, stables, smithies, and armories lined the inner walls of the fortress. At its center was a square tower, probably a hundred and thirty feet tall if Silas had to guess, built from the local sandstone. A narrow staircase about ten feet tall led to a drawbridge that allowed people entry to the keep. Silas had to slow as he climbed the stairs, which were without handrail and clearly designed to prevent attackers from gaining easy access. At the top of the stairs, a spearman, far more alert than any of his fellows had been, raised a quizzical eyebrow when Silas climbed the last stair.

"Pray pardon," Silas said, pausing to catch his breath. He

really was getting far too old for this sort of thing. "I am looking for the garrison commander, I have a message to deliver." It felt half-baked when he said it, but on the spot it seemed the best thing to say that wouldn't arouse suspicion. At least it would raise less questions than, "Hey, some nixie told me you need to stop dumping poison in the river or they're liable to get mad about it."

The guard gave Silas a once over, evaluating his appearance. Silas debated if he should have changed into some of his more mystical looking robes that at least had a touch of embroidery. Instead he was wearing homespun traveling clothes, designed to wear well and resist exposure to the elements. At least Silas's carved rowan-wood staff, etched with arcane runes, looked somewhat official. "Head up two flights, then for the main chamber. If she ain't there you can give your message to her steward. You carrying bronze?" A shake of the head from Silas was apparently good enough for the guard. "All right then." The guard spat into the empty space beside the drawbridge and that seemed the end of the conversation.

Silas walked into the keep and was pleasantly surprised to find rather than a dark and damp interior, the castle was lit with spheres of magical light spaced at regular intervals. He imagined the savings on candles and rush lights alone justified the hassle of getting mages to install the lights in the first place. He walked down a hallway, which was strangely silent, the hubbub of outside muffled by the thick stone walls of the tower. Up a spiral staircase, past first landing and into the second, he finally heard the sounds of other people. There was a heated argument that could be heard echoing from down the hallway to his right, so he followed it until he came to a set of open double doors.

The room beyond probably took up most of the floor, if Silas's calculations were correct. Long wooden trestle tables crowded the interior, arranged in a U-shape around the room. In less busy days, Silas assumed this was where the garrison commander held feasts to honor any imperial dignitaries of note who passed through, but for now it was in use as an administrative office. Dozens of scribes were seated at the tables, carefully answering to correspondence or doing the inevitable paperwork that always seemed to come with the business of empire. Page girls, anywhere from seven to fourteen years old, ran back and forth carrying message to and from other locations in the fortress. At what would have been the high table, where the castellan and her personal retinue would sit during a feast, Silas saw a scale model of a completed fortress. Several adult women stood around, so engrossed in their argument they did not notice when Silas approached.

"I'm telling you, we can't build walkers fast enough to meet your demands," said one woman, wearing the traditional purple sash of an arcane engineer around her waist. Those involved in the manufacture of magical devices tended to avoid fancy robes due to the hands-on nature of their work, and this woman was no exception. "The majority of our capacity is going towards the military quotas. Any spare capacity is earmarked for bronze-working. No bronze, no walkers. Simple as that."

"And I'm telling you there isn't enough labor for us to keep building at the rate the castellan wants," replied another woman, this one wearing the traditional leather apron of a mistress mason with her compass and square at her belt. "I've got plenty of masons for the dressing and finishing, yes, but we don't have enough raw material. We're only able to go as fast as we can because we have a stockpile of stone on hand. Give us five walkers and we'd have all the stone we need."

"Five?!" a second woman wearing a leather apron – who, based on the number of burn marks on her face, was probably in charge of the bronzesmiths – exclaimed. "I've only got six as is! And we're barely meeting quota! You take five of ours and I guarantee we'll fall behind; *nothing* works in this city without bronze. And who will explain that to the next imperial legate?"

"All right, all right, you've all made your points." This was said by a harried-looking woman in a green robe who carried an oversized silver key on her belt, the symbol of a steward. When Silas looked at her, there was something strangely familiar about her. "Emeline, how many walkers do you have set to come on line within the next fortnight?"

The arcane engineer pulled out a wax tablet from her pocket and consulted it. "We should be able to finish another three, possibly five if we pull extra shifts. That would give us two above quota."

"Béatrice, if I were to pull two walkers from your work crews, how much would that upset bronze production for the next fortnight?"

Béatrice pulled out a wooden slide rule and did some quick calculations. "We would have a shortfall of approximately five hundred pounds. Which would mean…"

"That you would be comfortably above quota with three tonnes for the month already. Séverine, you'll get two walkers to help you quarry the stone, but that's all we can spare for right now. Any excess capacity is still going to go to the bronze. Emeline, let your arcanists know I will approve extra money for the shifts they're going to have to pull." It was clear nobody was happy with this arrangement but it ended the argument. The three craftswomen departed and the steward finally noticed Silas. "Silas! How nice of you to drop in! Sorry, the place is a bit of a mess right now, as you can see. Is Bundersnoot up to his old tricks?"

The coin finally dropped for Silas and he remembered why the steward looked so familiar. She had inherited Robèrta's piercing blue eyes. "You're Alayna. Alayna Walpole. Robèrta's little girl. I haven't seen you in, what, twenty years?"

"More or less, but who's counting?" What brings you to my neck of the woods these days?"

Stunned by the coincidence, Silas could only say the first thing that came to mind. "You're not going to believe this, but some nixie are mad that you're dumping poison in their river."

* * *

"There's a new empress-regent on the throne, Grâce X. Despite the popularity of the Cascade family, there are some who are questioning if they backed the right horse. The Cascades have focused on consolidating their hold on the core lands but that's come at the expense of the periphery. And more than one great family's wealth depended on the periphery. So Grâce X is trying to reassert control beyond the Braelors, which is why we're doing this." Alayna gestured towards the hive of activity below them. She had taken Silas up to the roof of the tower where they could look down at Coursuperieur in its entirety. From his vantage point, Silas got the impression he was looking into the bowels of hell.

"But that's coming with a cost," Silas said. "The devastation could make this entire valley uninhabitable for decades to come, perhaps centuries. Surely you must see that."

ACROSS AMASTICA

"Oh, everyone sees it," Alayna agreed. "I see it, the workers see it, even Governor-General Cascade in her infinite wisdom sees it, not that she'd admit it. But it's not like there's anything we can *do* about it."

"But you're her steward, surely you could tell people to…"

"Do what, Silas?" Alayna snapped at Silas, anger flashing in her eyes. "Mine less ore? Cut less trees? Make less bronze? We're under Imperial Edict here, if we don't meet the Empress-regent's demands she'll just replace us with somebody who will. So I do my job to the best of my ability and if I can contain the damage, I will. But that's all I can promise."

Silas frowned, his arguments dying on his lips. Everyone knew this wasn't sustainable, but they didn't see any other options. The people in real power, the people who could make this stop with a few words, didn't care about the consequences they just wanted their bronze. An accident of family had allowed Silas to at least speak to Alayna, but there would be no such coincidence that would guarantee his access to the halls of power in Tevioch.

Alayna looked a little embarrassed by her outburst. "Listen, there's some things we can try. I can order the smelters to keep their slag away from the river. We can try to plant more trees after we clear-cut. I'll toss some ideas around. Small things. Maybe it'll help?"

"Possibly," Silas agreed, looking out at the industrial sprawl below him. It was drawing near sunset and the furnaces still glowed with activity. Not even the arrival of night would stop the forges of Coursuperieur. "I'll see if the nixie have any suggestions for what you can do. Thank you for meeting with me, at least."

"Anything for one of mom's old adventuring buddies! Hey,

would you want to stay in the fortress? I could probably get you a billet if you'd like. Probably far more comfortable than whatever inn you're currently staying in."

"No, that's quite all right. We've already got the horses stabled and I hate to move them again so soon. Especially after traveling on the river." The lie came easily for Silas. The truth was, the sheer number of soldiers made him uncomfortable. He'd been on the opposite side of the Cascades, very briefly and not terribly enthusiastically he'd admit, but still the opposing side. The wizards who ruled the Empire had long memories and didn't particularly care if Silas had been a reluctant rebel who had merely followed his teacher. That level of grudge factored heavily in Silas's decision to settle in independent Elade-voc. "If we need anything else, I'll be sure to let you know."

Silas took his leave of Alayna and made his way back out of the fortress, wrapped in his own melancholy thoughts. The streets were filled with workers – both the dirty, exhausted crowd who were stumbling home from their shifts at the belching furnaces and their slightly cleaner, slightly less exhausted replacements trudging towards their next shift. Silas could not help but feel overwhelmed by the futility of his quest. What could he, one wizard, possibly do to stop the inexorable advance of empire?

Eventually he found his way back to the inn and slowly climbed the stairs to their rented room. When he opened the door, he found Waif waiting for him, eating a bowl of pottage he assumed came from downstairs. "I managed to get the horses and wagon taken care of. As far as I know, all our possessions are where they need to be. Did you have any luck?"

"Not as much as I'd like. Any more of that pottage?" Waif

handed up a second bowl that was still warm and Silas grunted as he sat down on his bedroll. "The steward turned out to be the daughter of an old friend, but we can't rely on her for help. I'll have to see if I can meet with the nixie again, they might have some suggestions. Waif, do you mind getting that?" This last sentence was in response to a persistent thudding at the door to their room. Waif opened it to reveal Bundersnoot, who sauntered in with a piece of roasted duck in his mouth.

"Did you even leave the inn or have you spent the entire time begging in the kitchen again?" Silas asked. There was a mumbled response from Bundersnoot. "Don't talk with your mouth full!"

Bundersnoot walked over to Waif's now-empty bowl and put his prize down. "Well, do you want me to answer or not? You ask me a question without even giving me a chance to put my dinner down, *which I had to arrange for myself*, and then get mad when I *do* answer. I swear, I don't know why I put up with you."

"Bundersnoot," Silas's tone was plaintive, clearly tired of arguing. "I have had a very discouraging day and I have to tell the nixie I have no idea how to solve their problem."

"Well, fortunately for you *I* may have a solution." Bundersnoot managed to look even more proud of himself than usual with this announcement. "I did manage to go speak with the cats in the city and they filled me in on some local history. So, it turns out about ten years ago some prospectors were out in the mountains seeing if there was anything valuable. And guess what they found."

"Gold?" Waif asked.

"The end to your boundless appetite?" Silas asked.

"No." Bundersnoot refused to be baited. "They found both

copper *and* tin. In the same place."

Silas blinked in surprise and simply said, "Oh."

"I don't understand," Waif said. "Why is that important?"

"To make bronze, you need both copper and tin," Silas explained. "I mean, you can use arsenic or other metals but most of the time it's tin. The problem is that copper and tin are seldom found in the same place."

"Exactly," Bundersnoot said, taking over the explanation. "Which means if you're going to make bronze, you usually have to import copper, or more usually tin from somewhere else. It's a huge pain but that's why the Empire invested so heavily in things like the roads and the paddlewheelers. They need trade to be able to flow if they're going to get the resources they need. And as a result, their bronze production has always been decentralized. But with *both* of the resources in the same place they can make all the bronze they need. And between the river and the highway leading back to Tevioch, it's a perfect distribution hub."

"Better and better," Silas grumbled. "And with Grâce having ambitions on bringing the borderlands more firmly under the Imperial aegis…"

"Yeah, I found out about that too. We *really* should warn Lady Gavreau about that." Bundersnoot paused to take some bites out of his piece of duck. "Fortunately, I think there might be a way for us to stop this. We go to the oréade."

"Well, I can't imagine they'd be happy about all the devastation either," Silas said. "But what would we ask them to do?" Bundersnoot told him and Silas had to admit he was impressed. "You know, that may not be a terrible idea. Bundersnoot, you've done excellent work today. Remind me to buy you some fresh chicken tomorrow."

Bundersnoot looked up from his dinner, his eyes wide with shock. "Silas, is your curse acting up again? Because that sounded like a compliment. Waif, was that a compliment?"

"That was definitely a compliment," Waif agreed.

"And a promise of fresh chicken. I *love* fresh chicken. If I've died and gone to kitty heaven, nobody tell me."

Silas merely chuckled as he gave Bundersnoot an affectionate head rub.

* * *

The next night, they hiked into the mountains surrounding town, following a dirt trail up to an abandoned mine. Scattered around the entrance to the mine were discarded pieces of broken equipment, not even worth the effort of salvaging them. The night was overcast, blocking light from the moon and stars which helped hide their expedition from prying eyes. All traces of the great forests that had once covered these mountains were gone so Silas kept the sphere of light he summoned dim and low to the ground to keep from revealing their presence.

"The cats said they sank this mine about eight years ago, when the Empire started really working on expanding. They dug pretty deep into the mountain but they never found anything worth the effort, so they ended up closing it. Still lots of small mammals that live inside it, if you're into that sort of thing I guess."

The mine did not exactly look welcoming. Nobody had bothered to do maintenance on the abandoned structure and some of the support props sagged dangerously. Fortunately, that was probably the most dangerous thing about this particular mine. Silas recalled the time he and Bundersnoot had to go into a mine with Narses, Gerald, and Robèrta after a particularly large and ill-tempered salamander. And this wasn't one of the forest salamanders, which were fairly mundane creatures that liked to live in ponds and streams even if they were absurdly poisonous. No, this had been one of the large, fire-breathing salamanders which could grow larger than an ox and eat people if they got a taste for it. For not the first time in his life, Silas wondered how the same name could apply to two vastly different creatures and whether maybe changing the name of one of them might be a good idea.

No, this mine wouldn't have any such dangerous creatures living within it, but there was something about it which made Silas feel strange. Something about going down into the earth that felt weirdly *right* to him. He felt his arm start to throb, and there was almost a pull towards the damp darkness of the land below that weighed on his mind. He thought it would be silly to admit it but all the same, the feeling was there. When they got back to the inn he was definitely applying another treatment of lunar caustic.

About three hundred feet into the mine they found a chamber were three tunnels branched off, the one to the right sealed off by rockfall the other two stretching distantly under the mountain. "Which way do we go?" asked Waif.

"I think we're far enough in that we can try asking them to meet with us." Silas unshouldered the satchel of supplies he had brought and opened it carefully. "The oréade don't like to travel to the surface if they can avoid it and they're more likely to answer an invitation if you do it underground." Silas withdrew five white wax candles and placed them in a circle on the ground, lighting each with a spark of wytchfyre. He then retrieved a fresh loaf of bread, a small crock of honey, and a collection of amethyst crystals he had found in a market stall in Coursuperieur. He placed them in the center of the circle and Bundersnoot paced around the circle, imbuing it with magical power. Finally Silas knelt at the edge of the circle and patted the ground for Waif to join him.

"Are we going to do a summoning?" Waif asked, their eyes eager to learn more about the secrets of magic. They'd been more enthusiastic about the whole endeavor ever since their last talk with Silas. They had spent most of their free time practicing their control of magical energies and while Waif still hadn't mastered controlling a light spell, they kept asking Silas where they could improve. Silas did his best to guide Waif and even when their spells fell apart Waif refused to get discouraged.

"This isn't exactly a summoning so much as it's an invitation to come talk," Silas answered. "If it were a summoning we would have to take greater safety precautions."

"Well, what's the difference between the two?"

"Summoning involves calling something from the Land of the Fae into our world here. This is very dangerous because the things that live there are, well, they don't think like you and me. Their behavior is erratic at the best of times. You have to take many, many precautions when dealing with them lest they harm you.

"The oréade, however, are much like the nixie. They're part of both our world and the Land of the Fae. The result is they're a little more...grounded. Their motives are usually more comprehensible than other creatures. It's unlikely they'll attack us without provocation."

"And the bread and crystals?" Waif asked.

"Just because a magical creature is friendly or at least neutral towards you doesn't mean it's not good manners to bring a gift. Especially if you intend to impose upon their hospitality. All right, now I want you to focus."

Waif closed their eyes and put all their attention to their breathing. Taking in a long, deep breath, holding it, and then slowly releasing it. Silas waited until he could sense they had quieted their mind. Granted, a turbulent adolescent's mind was *never* completely quiet, but it was much closer now. "All right, I want you to think about earth and stone. How it smells, how it feels, what it sounds like. How it tastes."

"How it tastes?" Waif had not opened their eyes but one eyebrow was cocked in confusion. "Just because I grew up dirt poor doesn't mean we ate dirt."

"Salt is a rock, and don't sass me, child. Just get a good sensory image of it in your mind. As many senses as you can use."

Waif retreated into their mind and went over their scant years of life. They thought about how dirt roads could be soft and warm underfoot in the summer, easy to walk over, and how that same dirt could become cold and sucking mud with a sudden rainstorm. They thought about the rough texture of the stone walls of Silas's shop, how it would turn cold in winter but provide a reassuring bulk in the dark of night. Of the smooth, round stones weathered by the river that they used to hunt with their siblings down at the riverbank in Bridgegate. The very different sounds the cobbles outside their shop made, whether they were trodden on by a horse or by someone in wooden shoes. Waif even managed to imagine the smell in the air when a hard rain came down in Elade-voc, quenching the stones of the city and releasing an undefinable scent in the air. And then they felt a nudge at their elbow.

ACROSS AMASTICA

"You did an excellent job," Bundersnoot said, looking up at Waif, his glass-green eyes glowing in the candlelight. Waif looked up to see three women standing across the circle. Like the nixie, there was an ethereal beauty to them, but the similarities ended there. The oréade varied wildly in skin tones. One was the pale gray of granite, another the rich dark brown of soil, a third the bright red of clay. The gray one's hair looked like moss or lichen, a deep green that trailed down their back in long strand, but the hair of the brown and red ones looked like the fibers of tiny roots, ranging in color from pale brown to white. They were all dressed in simple dun tunics made from roughspun linen.

"We have come as you asked," said the pale gray one, her voice sounding like two stones scraping together. She and her sisters knelt across from them and the red one picked up the bread and honey, sharing it with the brown one. "We appreciate your gifts of hospitality. For too long humans have plundered our realm, taking our gifts and giving no thanks. We have watched our cousins sicken as poisons leach into their sacred river, and yet the humans take no notice. It is a grave imbalance."

The gray oréad stopped her speech to pick up one of the amethyst stones and looked at it critically before she gave it a quick lick. Joy overcame her face and she popped the amethyst into her mouth. There was a crunch as she chewed on the stone, loud enough to make the two humans and cat wince. The gray oréad smiled. "It has been a long time since I've had a silicate quite that delicious. You'll have to tell me where you found it."

"I would be more than happy to," Silas said. "As I'm sure you have already guessed, our presence here is not merely social in nature. Your cousins asked us to help them and we have come

142

up with a solution but we need your help. We want to move the tin."

The oréade looked confused at this suggestion. "We are not sure what you mean by this. We know the ores that contain tin are very valuable to the humans of Coursuperieur. They go to great efforts to find it, overcome by greed they dig ever deeper into our mountains. If we were to hide it how could we keep them from finding it?"

Silas took out a piece of chalk and found a convenient flat rock to draw on. He drew a circle next to a wavy line. "This is Coursuperieur next to the Ganorne, where they're doing all the mining and smelting." He drew some chevrons surrounding the city. "And these are the mountains that they're mining from. But they can only really afford to take the copper and the tin from the mountains nearby." Silas drew a circle around it and drew more chevrons. "If you moved the tin far enough away from the river, say fifty miles or so, it would be too expensive in terms of energy for them to get the tin to where it needs to be smelted. Furthermore, if you keep it deep, hidden away where nobody can just stumble upon it, they won't know where to start looking."

"We cannot move that much tin," the gray oréad said, sorrow in her voice. "Perhaps, in another age, we could have worked such great wonders. But now, even if all our sisters labored, we could at best move the tin deeper into the mountain, make it harder to find and seem as if their mines have been exhausted."

"Then we do that," Silas said, "but we make everyone *think* you've moved it hundreds of miles away. After all, if the spirits of earth and stone say there will be no tin to be found, who's going to contradict them?"

The oréade gathered together, whispering in voices so low

that not even Bundersnoot could hear them. For several minutes they seemed to argue back and forth, debating the merits of Silas's plan. Eventually they all faced the humans again and the gray one spoke. "This, perhaps we could do."

* * *

"Can we go get something to eat? I'm starving," Bundersnoot whined.

Silas produced a piece of roast chicken and Bundersnoot pounced on it hungrily. They were waiting at the landing, watching as boats were loaded and unloaded in a frenzy of activity. Across the river, the furnaces continued to burn as men dumped their loads of crushed ore. Business appeared to be going as usual, which was perfect for their plan. "The nixie and oréade should be making their move soon."

As if on cue, the waters of the Ganorne started to rise. At first so slowly that nobody who wasn't looking for it would notice. But soon, the river's swell overcame the landing, turning the muddy riverbank into a swamp. Across the river the waters surged towards the furnaces and great jets of steam rose where the water met the heat of the fires. The workers screamed in shock and fled, unwilling to become scalded to death or drown.

Silas could see further up that the river had flooded out smithies and other businesses, rapidly overcoming the buildings that were jammed in wherever space could be found. The results were suitably dramatic, with workers fleeing uphill away from the water. "That should be enough to get the steward's attention. Possibly even the governor herself." White-cloaked soldiers attempted to reinstate order and manage the evacuation, with mixed results. Most people paid them no heed in their headlong flight to escape. Those that stopped were press-ganged into helping with the flood control efforts, which at this point consisted of keeping people from going into the river since there was nothing they could do to stop the advance of the waters.

Word spread up the chain of command quickly because Alayna and a woman who definitely looked like the local governor came storming down towards the riverbanks. Although what good two more people would have done in such a catastrophe was very little. For a solid fifteen minutes, the government of Coursuperieur milled about with no idea what they could actually *do* about this sudden and unprecedented flood. They were so busy arguing that none of them noticed the waters slowly receding nor the women with kelp green hair emerging from the waters.

"For too long our hospitality has been abused by the humans," said the nixie in unison. With the benefit of some magical voice projection their message was clearly audible throughout the entirety of the city. "You have traveled on our rivers, benefited from our gifts, taken of our bounty. And how do you repay us? With poison!" As one the nixie pointed towards the piles of slag accumulated near the shore. "You give us no thanks but rather condemn us to a slow death. Is this proper?"

While the humans were still reeling from the nixie's challenge, the oréade appeared on cue, rising from the earth. There were dozens of them, every oréad from miles around had answered the call for aid. "We also have been slighted," they said as one. Their voices were as inexorable as a rockslide, able to shake bones with their resonance. "You have taken our gifts, but have we been repaid? You humans have dug deeper into our mountains, searching for every last scrap of treasure that could be found. You have hollowed out our mountains without a thought for we who live in them. And then, insult of insults, you use our gifts to poison our cousins.

"We cannot allow this to continue. From this day forth we decree no tin nor copper shall be found in our mountains. Despite your labor and toil, all your mines shall become barren, offering only stone. Thus shall it be until proper respect is once again offered to us, the spirits of this world."

And with that their speech ended. The oréade abruptly disappeared back into the earth, leaving no trace of their passing. The nixie all turned into otters and dove beneath the river's surface, swimming away before anyone could react.

Oddly enough, the majority of the city seemed confused by the announcement. It had been a strange interlude in an otherwise normal day and they quickly returned to the mundane everyday business that consumed their lives. From this far away, it was difficult for Silas to make out too many details but it was clear Alayna was furious. Silas started walking in her direction and Bundersnoot followed, protesting the entire way.

"Silas! Shouldn't we be quickly and quietly making our way *out* of the city? Silas? Waif, he's not listening, see if you can get him to listen. Silas!"

"There is little point in us attempting to flee. Alayna will simply deploy the troops stationed here and drag us back, possibly imprisoning us, and causing unreasonable delay. Bundersnoot, stop whining."

"I'm not whining, I'm simply raising valid concerns," Bundersnoot said.

They approached the knot of imperial officials and Alayna

saw them approaching. "You!" she shouted, pointing an accusatory finger towards Silas in particular. "This is *your* fault! Guards, arrest this man!" Two imperial troops strode forward but Silas refused to be intimidated. He summoned a shield of pale green light, which shimmered around him, Waif, and Bundersnoot, and repelled the soldiers.

"I delivered their message and you chose to ignore it," Silas answered calmly. "I informed them of your choice and they took what action seemed best. I cannot be held responsible for their decision." A lie, of course, seeing as he had given them the idea in the first place, but Alayna didn't need to know that.

"Steward, who is this man?" A woman dressed in violet robes with a golden chain of office around her neck joined the conversation. Clearly the city's governor, probably a member of the Cascade family if Silas had to guess.

"Your Excellency," Silas bowed. "I am the wizard Silas. I spoke with your steward a few days ago to deliver a message from the nixie of Ganorne, who asked me to speak on their behalf. She informed me there was little she could do about their requests and I passed that message back."

"And what happened here today?" The governor gestured towards the water-damaged buildings which had been flooded by the nixie manipulation of the river.

Silas paused. His first impulse was to be flippant. As an experienced wizard he had grown accustomed to tweaking the nose of authority because they lacked any real power to strike back. Lady Gavreau and the Council of Elders were merchants and politicians but they weren't wizards. But in the Empire, magical ability and authority went hand in hand. This woman would not have been given control of a city as important as Coursuperieur without being a potent magic-wielder in her own right. Very likely she had as much or even more experience than Silas, and who knows how many family magical secrets at her disposal.

"Your Excellency, the nixie and the oréade hoped to avoid such extreme measures but my failure made their choice inevitable. They deeply regret this state of affairs, as do I, but they were left with no choice. If you wish to negotiate with them, I will gladly pass the message along, but that is a decision that only you can make. It is entirely within your power what happens next."

This governor didn't immediately start calling down lightning or summoning wytchfyre to immolate Silas on the spot, so he concluded the answer had been respectful enough. "I shall consult with my advisors before giving my answer. How shall I find you?"

"Sadly, urgent business takes me elsewhere for now. But if one remembers the old ways, I am certain you could reach the nixie and oréade easily enough."

"And if I were to detain you at my pleasure?"

Silas spread his arms and shrugged, taking refuge in the truth. "Then I may die in your custody. That is the nature of my business."

The governor frowned, dissatisfied with this answer. "Very well, master Silas, you have my leave to go. But you have drawn the attention of the Empire today, I would advise against any action which would bring further scrutiny."

"By your leave, Your Excellency." Silas bowed again and stepped back respectfully, leaving Alayna and the governor to debate their next moves.

"Well that went fairly well, all things considered," Silas said when they were safely out of earshot. "I haven't been arrested and we can leave without harassment."

"I still think we should have just left, let the imperial bureaucracy sort out their own problems." Bundersnoot grumbled. He jumped up onto the wagon and found a comfortable spot to start napping in. "But does anyone listen to me? No, of course not. What do I know? Not like I found the solution to this crisis while you were all stumbling about without a clue as to what to do next."

Silas sighed. "Yes, Bundersnoot, you are the cleverest cat in all of creation. Truly the smartest, wittiest cat without whom I would barely be able to lace up my boots in the morning. There, are you satisfied?"

"A little more food wouldn't go awry," Bundersnoot said and Silas booped him on the nose.

"You know, a particularly clever cat would find the rest of the roast chicken I had stored in the wagon. If he was really the cleverest cat in all creation." Silas said, trying and failing to keep a straight face. Bundersnoot frowned, not understanding his words at first and then let out a happy meow and dove into the collected luggage. Soon the sound of a happy cat eating came from somewhere within the wagon.

"So what do we do now?" Waif asked, climbing up beside Silas in the front of the wagon.

"Brief stop to consult with the nixie and oréade. The solution we've gone with won't solve everything overnight. It's going to take time for the poisons to be removed from the Ganorne, and I don't know how long that will take. We've at least managed to keep things from getting worse, though. And after that?" Silas took up the reins and clicked his tongue, getting the horses into motion. "We head towards Tevioch."

Somewhere Near Tevioch

The warm spring sun was high in the sky and Bundersnoot was enjoying every minute of it. He reveled in the delicious warmth as the wagon traveled on an imperial highway. The highways were crafted long ago with magics either well-hidden or long forgotten, ribbons of black stone that ran ruler-straight through the countryside. There was no jolting or bumping through ruts or potholes on a road like this, just a smooth, uninterrupted ride that one could peacefully sleep through. Almost everything a cat could ask for. If only he wasn't so hungry.

"When are we stopping for lunch?" He raised his head to look at Silas and Waif, who were riding in the front.

"We're not," Silas said without even looking back at Bundersnoot. "We're making good time and I don't want to stop. If you're hungry, you can always have some of the jerky."

Bundersnoot crinkled his face in disgust. "That jerky you bought is indistinguishable from leather. Very old, very tough leather at that. I don't know how you can keep eating it."

Silas said nothing. He had become increasingly withdrawn as they came closer to Tevioch. They were coming close to the end of this quest and, hopefully, a cure for the curse of the vampire that still afflicted him. The lunar caustic had helped but its efficacy was beginning to wane. The black lines radiating from the wound he had taken a year ago were advancing towards his shoulder, undeterred by any of the treatments he applied. He could tell time was running out, and if they didn't find a unicorn in time then, well...

Silas's mind turned to the stinger of the manticore still wrapped safely in a leather bundle. There was always that option which would ensure he would never rise again as one of the living dead.

"Look over there!" Waif pointed excitedly at a column of imperial cavalry coming towards them on the road. "Unicorns!" Silas pulled on the reins and steered the horses to the side of the road, giving the cavalry plenty of space to pass. Waif looked at the cavalry with awed enthusiasm. The unicorns all had snowy white coats, so well brushed that they glowed in the sunlight, and each mount was a mass of well-defined muscle. These were cavalry that would not blow out or tire during battle, a decisive factor in many of the empire's wars. And in the center of each creature's forehead, exactly halfway between their eyes, was the legendary black horn.

Their riders were armored in gleaming bronze, each with a high helmet with a long, trailing purple horsehair plume. These were the elite of the empire's forces and they knew it, riding as if all the world belonged to them. The officers carried themselves in restrained dignity, the cream of the empire's lower nobility who had made careers of the imperial military. The troopers joked and sang amongst themselves, as if they were simply headed out for a picnic and every day would be this fine. They didn't so much as glance in Silas's direction; all who made way for them were beneath notice.

"Why didn't you ask them for help?" Waif asked after the

151

column had passed and they made their way back onto the road. "Don't you need a unicorn to help heal you?"

"I do," Silas said. "But I need a *true* unicorn, not an imperial one."

"Well what's the difference?"

"Imperial unicorns are magically enhanced horses, specially bred to be the perfect cavalry mount. They are larger, stronger, and more resilient than any ordinary horse. Their horn, which only begins to grow in after their first year, is wickedly sharp and as hard as diamond. These are creatures which are meant to kill rather than heal."

"Oh." Waif was momentarily stunned by the bluntness of Silas's statement. "And a true unicorn?"

"More than just a horse with a horn, I can tell you that," Bundersnoot said, abandoning his nap for now. "The obvious physical identifiers are cloven hooves, a beard, and a tail like a lion. But imperial unicorns have been stamped on so many coins that most people don't know the difference." They passed a stone marker on the road that said "Tevioch 50 Miles" and Bundersnoot squinted at it like it had personally offended him. "How much closer to the capital do we need to get, Silas?"

"Close enough that we can find a unicorn," Silas said and Bundersnoot gave a growl of frustration.

"We're not exactly welcome among imperial authorities, especially after Coursuperieur. They've probably already got a message to the current empress-regent."

"I know, I know." Silas pulled the wagon over to the side of the road and put his head in his hands. "The truth is, I'm scared. More scared than at any point before when we started this quest. I'm constantly plagued by doubts. What if Isidore was completely wrong and there is *no* cure for this curse?" Silas

SOMEWHERE NEAR TEVIOCH

pointed towards his arm, covered by his sleeve but he felt like the entire world could see the creeping poison. "I've dragged us halfway across Amastica to find an answer, and at best I have maybe one chance in three of this working. If we can even find a unicorn."

Wordlessly, Bundersnoot climbed into Silas's lap and began purring, exuding an aura of emotional warmth and stability. Waif leaned up against Silas and hugged him like a child would hug their parent. "I'm sure we can find a unicorn. After all, we managed to find a manticore. And they're loads more dangerous than unicorns." Waif paused, considering this statement. "Unicorns *are* less dangerous than manticores, right?"

Silas chuckled and ruffled Waif's hair affectionately. "Yes, everything I've ever read says that unicorns are gentle-natured and we will be in no danger unless we try to harm them. And only someone incredibly ambitious or incredibly stupid tries to harm a unicorn."

"Amazing how those two traits coincide," Bundersnoot said, stopping his purr to look up at Silas. "But where are we going to find a young, female virgin? Preferably with hair as dark and lustrous as a raven's wing, skin as rich as chestnut, her eyes sparkling in the sun—"

"Yes, yes," Silas cut Bundersnoot's description off. "You know perfectly well that's part folk myth and part imperial propaganda. If we approach respectfully there's no reason a unicorn won't at least give us a fair hearing." There was a little cat laugh at Silas's frustration that he chose to ignore.

"What was Bundersnoot talking about?" Waif asked.

"So, little history lesson for you. Way, way back, some fifteen hundred years ago, the Empress and her armies of elven

153

warriors emerged from the Land of Fae and took our world by storm. For three hundred years, she expanded her empire, covering much of the continent of Amastica. The most elite of these soldiers were her unicorn cavalry, much like the band of warriors that just passed us on the road."

"Now, in the very early days, her cavalry rode true unicorns. But as time went on, these unicorns escaped and managed to avoid being recaptured, which led to the magical breeding program that made the imperial unicorns. The Empress being the Empress, she heavily favored women in the ranks of these elite units, especially her daughters and granddaughters. And while I don't want to make disparaging comments towards the Faeborn family—"

"Gods forfend you do such a thing," Bundersnoot said.

"—some of them were, let's say they were extremely interested in glamouring their appearance. So a lot of people saw some very beautiful women riding around on unicorns, and bards being bards, they wrote a lot of poems and songs about women and unicorns."

"Her eyes they sparkled like amber/ That jewel so bright and fair/ They shined so in the sunlight/ Just like her lustrous hair—" Bundersnoot recited and Silas gave him a bop on the head. "Ouch! What was that for?"

"To clarify, bards wrote a lot of *bad* poems and songs about women and unicorns, and certain cats should *not* recite them where I can hear them. Just because Gerald had terrible taste in poetry doesn't mean I have to keep suffering for it."

Waif laughed. "Whatever happened to the true unicorns, then?" they asked.

"A lot of the true unicorns escaped back into the Land of Fae, the barriers between worlds were weaker in the Empress's time. But some of them remained behind and every now and then people would catch glimpses of them, most frequently near the core imperial realms around Tevioch. Granted, it's been about a hundred years since anyone's last seen one but I suppose it's try or die."

"If you die I will be extremely put out," Bundersnoot said, not looking up from his place in Silas's lap. "I will teach Waif everything I know about necromancy to bring you back from the dead just to make sure I am fed on time."

"Everything you know about necromancy could fill a thimble," Silas retorted. "Besides, I thought you were training Waif to feed you regularly."

Bundersnoot huffed. "*Someone*, and I mention no names you understand, but *someone* has been a *very* bad influence on Waif and has taught them that sometimes when I ask to be fed I should be ignored. Ignored! As if I, Bundersnoot, would ever *lie* about needing to be fed! It's a disgrace, an absolute disgrace. As if a cat such as myself, a respected pillar of the community—" Silas managed to stifle a laugh but only barely "— would stoop to *lying* about matters of life and death! Honestly I have no idea what the world has come to."

Silas reached down and gave Bundersnoot's head a good rub. "Indeed, dark days are definitely ahead for us all if a cat such as yourself can't be trusted."

Bundersnoot purred for a moment and then batted Silas's hand away. "But to return to my original point, you're not allowed to die. I forbid it."

Silas smiled but winced when he felt the wound in his arm twinge. "Well, Bundersnoot, here's hoping the universe bends to your whim."

ACROSS AMASTICA

* * *

Their journey through the countryside was largely uneventful. The imperial road was busy with traffic: teamsters driving wagons to market that were so heavy-laden that their axles groaned from the weight, patrols of imperial cavalry mounted on mundane horses keeping the peace and discouraging bandits, and the occasional gilded carriage of an aristocrat either heading towards the city from their country estate or the other way around. As a perpetual city-dweller, Silas never remembered the complicated seasonal migrations of the rich and powerful, and frankly couldn't be bothered to care.

The countryside itself consisted of well-maintained lands, alternating between fields of grain or peas and pastures filled with sheep or cattle. It was all so very picturesque as the farmers went about, paying the people on the road no attention whatsoever. It was a stark contrast from his last time through these lands. After deserting the Silverbark cause, he and Bundersnoot had traveled furtively, remaining far away from the main roads and the clashing armies. Hardly a soul could be seen in the countryside, so many had fled from the devastation to the protection of fortified settlements. Any people he did see were at a distance and long gone before he approached, fearing bandits or worse. The fields and pastures remained barren, anything edible having long since been carted off by someone. What a change two decades of peace made.

Late in the afternoon they came to the market town of Autumnglade, one of the many towns where the produce of the countryside was gathered before being shipped to feed the hungry populace of Tevioch. Autumnglade was a riot of buying and selling. Here, a stockyard where cattle were

156

SOMEWHERE NEAR TEVIOCH

examined before auction. There a farmer driving a bargain with a bronze merchant on new tools for her farm. And best of all, nobody gave Silas and Waif a second glance as they navigated the crowded streets.

Somehow, despite the crush of the crowd, they managed to find an inn to rest for the night. The landlady was preoccupied with the demands of her numerous other patrons to give Silas much inspection, she was more interested in if his money was any good than who he was or why he was traveling. A room for the night and food secured, they headed down to the busy common room to take their meal. Silas almost tripped on the last stair when a black cat streaked out from the kitchen and across his path. The cat turned and looked back at him, blinking its big yellow eyes once.

"Don't you take that attitude with him!" Bundersnoot said indignantly. "He's a wizard of the eight schools you know! He has as much a right to be here as you have!" The black cat meowed and tilted their head and somehow it looked... sassy? Bundersnoot definitely took offense. "Oh, you have got another thing coming, monsieur!"

In a move that surprised both Silas and Waif, Bundersnoot jumped from the stairs and landed directly on the black cat. The cats hissed as they tumbled over one another, trying to gain dominance. Bundersnoot tried to use his bulk to his advantage but the black cat was far too nimble and squirmed out from under him. The black cat ran off and Bundersnoot gave chase. "Hey! You get back here! I'm not done with you yet!"

Silas tried to stop his familiar from running off but Bundersnoot slipped through his hands and darted through the crowded room, disappearing in the crowd. The yowl of a cat and crash of crockery charted the course of the fleeing felines.

157

Silas sighed and gave up the pursuit. "He'll come back when he's finished whatever damn fool thing he's gotten into his head now," he said.

"He will?" Waif asked.

"He better, or he's going to find himself locked out of our room for the night. Come on, let's get some food." The inn offered a hearty pottage with enough spring onions and garlic to clear even the most stubborn of sinuses and plenty of fresh-baked bread, however Silas poked at his food listlessly. There were a couple small lumps of spring veal in his pottage but they were thoroughly cooked. He felt himself yearning for something rawer, where he could still taste the blood in the meat. Or better yet, why bother with the meat at all? Just drink the blood. Yes, he needed the blood. Blood. BLOOD-

"SILAS!"

Silas came to his senses and realized he was standing, a table knife in his hand and an extremely concerned Waif with both of their hands clutching his robe. "Sorry, lost in thought," Silas offered as way of explanation. "What's happening?"

"You got this really manic look on your face and then you picked up your knife and shot up all of a sudden. Silas, are you…are you all right?"

Embarrassed, Silas sat back down and put the knife back on the table. "No," Silas said. "No, I don't think I'm well at all."

* * *

Late that night Silas was woken by the sound of scratching at their door. Silas tumbled out of bed and managed to unlock the door to reveal an extremely satisfied Bundersnoot who sauntered in as if he was lord of all creation. "You look proud

SOMEWHERE NEAR TEVIOCH

of yourself, I take it you got the better of that poor black cat earlier?" Silas asked.

Bundersnoot smiled a fierce kitty smile, "I not only took on him, I took on his brother *and* his cousin. You are looking at the undisputed top tomcat of Autumnglade. *And* I got fed, not that you care."

Silas closed the door behind Bundersnoot and stooped down to rub the cat's head. "Something's gotten into you lately. You don't normally fight like that."

"It's for appearance's sake. Cats are more interested in hierarchy here in the imperial core. I can't just ask for information, I have to prove that I'm worthy. All very stupid and rather human in a way. But I *did* get some valuable information."

"Well don't leave me standing here all night," Silas said. "I'm an old man who needs his sleep."

Bundersnoot batted Silas's leg. "You always say that. Anyway word on the street is that there's a noble out here putting together a hunting party for a unicorn. A Comtesse d'Jumentpâturage. Apparently she's some big muckety-muck back at court and has a bee in her bonnet about capturing a true unicorn for the imperial stables. All of the cats are talking about it, even that Cinders bastard."

"But is it *true*?" Silas asked, hesitant to let himself really believe they could be so close to the end.

"Saw the hunting party myself. They were having a grand dinner in one of the larger houses here in town. They're setting out tomorrow morning to head for a patch of forest called Lightwood. There are reliable reports of a unicorn seen in that forest and the Comtesse wants to curry favor with the empress-regent. I think this might be our opportunity."

159

"Possibly," Silas said. "If we can find the unicorn before they do. Come on, let's get some sleep. We'll have an early march in the morning."

* * *

The good thing about nobility, Silas reflected, is that they very seldom get an early start in the morning. He was accustomed to rising with the dawn and after carrying Bundersnoot out of bed and a quick breakfast, they had gotten onto the road that would go closest to Lightwood within the hour. The Comtesse and her retinue, having partied well into the night, were still abed and only groggily made their way downstairs sometime closer to noon. Noble retinues also take considerable time to get going. Horses have to be saddled, servants marshaled, the best wines carefully packed with picnic lunches, and a thousand other fine details which made life so comfortable for the Amastican nobility. This meant that Silas was waiting to observe the nobles as they approached Lightwood Forest.

They had set up camp a small distance into the forest, and Silas had woven illusions around their camp to shield them from notice. Even a determined seeker schooled in the magic of illusions would have considerable difficulty finding their camp. They were watching the nobles begin setting up their own camp in an open pasture near the forest after the sheep residing in said pasture had been rudely evicted. Multiple great pavilions dyed in rich and gaudy colors were being erected by servants as the nobles stood around looking impressive with their armed retainers. There seemed to be around two hundred people in total in this hunting party.

"A big to-do and no mistake," Bundersnoot said. "Do you

SOMEWHERE NEAR TEVIOCH

want me to get closer and see what I can find out?"

"If you think you can sneak past those guards," Silas said. He didn't know much about the Comtesse d'Jumentpâturage but she seemed to believe in a bronze fist without the delicacy of the silk glove. There were at least twenty armed retainers visible, all of them equipped in fine bronze breastplates, greaves, and helmets. They patrolled the perimeter of the nobles' camp on their fine horses, not unicorns no but definitely among the best warhorses available in the empire. Each was armed with a lance, bronze sword, and a heavy-looking mace. Silas was a skilled wizard, yes, but a cadre of mounted warriors would pose a significant challenge.

Bundersnoot merely tsked and flicked his tail. "I've got more brains in my left front paw than those mounted brutes. Just watch me." Confidently Bundersnoot walked out of the forest and into the pasture heading directly for the patrolling knights. Amazingly, the knights did not see Bundersnoot approaching even though the grass which had been cropped nearly to the roots by the recently evicted sheep, provided no cover. Bundersnoot shot a look back at the hidden Silas and Waif and winked one of his glass green eyes saucily before walking right under a great bay warhorse. He tickled the horse's leg with his tail but the horse didn't even so much as snort.

"He's gilding the lily on that one. It'd serve him right if he got trampled," Silas muttered. He pulled out the tiger's eye charm and chanted the spell which would allow him to hear everything Bundersnoot heard as he infiltrated the imperial camp. Initially the only sounds were the hustle and bustle of camp life: orders being shouted at servants, the swearing of animal drovers, the whickers and snorts of horses. There was the shout of "Hey, that's not for you! You get back here!" and

161

Silas could only assume Bundersnoot had snatched some sort of treat from a cook and successfully absconded.

Finally they were able to pick out a specific conversation. "My lady, I really must advise against this expedition. Unicorns are known to be dangerous and even her Immortal Majesty, long may she reign, had difficulty bringing one to heel. To capture a unicorn, much less tame one, is a task even the greatest of the empress-regents found impossible."

"Yes, uncle," a young, confident female voice said. She had clearly heard this lecture many times before. "However, *I* must remind *you* that the fortunes of the Landfalls have fallen as late due to cousin Zéphyrine's bumbling." This was met by an indignant harrumph from her uncle. "If we are to advance our family within the court then I, as matriarch, must lead while the rest follow."

"Possession of a title does not grant you authority over our family, Lucette!" her uncle shouted. "My wife has as much right to lead and three decades of experience…"

"Three decades of experience simpering at the beck and call of even the lowest of the Cascades! By Her Immortal Majesty, no wonder they view us with scorn! Between your wife and your daughter it's a miracle we have any dignity left." It seemed Lucette's uncle was too stunned or too angry to muster a response. "No, we are doing it my way. It has been a year since mother died and it is well past time I take my place as head of this family. I have done my research and this will be our path forward. There *is* a unicorn in the Lightwood and I *will* be the one to capture it and bring it before the empress-regent. We will begin the hunt tomorrow."

"Very well," it was clear her uncle was biting out every word as if it had personally offended him. "Then, if you have no

SOMEWHERE NEAR TEVIOCH

further use of me, my lady, by your leave." There was a pause of about a minute and then he coughed.

"Yes, you're dismissed," Lucette said, as if her uncle were a servant slow on the uptake and had to be gently reminded.

Silas leaned back and gave a low whistle. "And I thought Elade-voc politics were bad. I suppose family and politics truly don't mix."

"So what do we do now?" Waif asked.

"Wait for Bundersnoot to come back, then we try searching the Lightwood. Maybe we'll get lucky and find the unicorn. If it hasn't already fled."

* * *

They did not get lucky. After several hours stumbling through the forest Silas had to call a halt as the sun started dipping towards the horizon. Waif had fallen into a thicket of nettles and had needed some quick healing magic, and Bundersnoot had slipped head-first into a stream which he had found both humiliating and unpleasant. Even Silas had felt like the forest was attacking him, personally, with every tripped-over root and snagged-on branch. Tired and frustrated, they returned to their campsite and had an unsatisfying meal of trail rations, made all the worse from the smells of roasted meat coming from the nobles' feast drifting on the wind a scant hundred feet away.

"What do we do tomorrow?" Bundersnoot asked. "I can scout, but I don't think even I can avoid them when they're beating every bush to see what comes out."

"The best thing we can do is stay put tomorrow, the illusions should nudge everyone away. Although how quickly they'll

163

get bored with this project I don't know. Maybe a few days, maybe a few weeks."

Bundersnoot looked up at Silas with concern. "I don't know if we have that much time to waste sitting around."

"I don't have any better ideas," Silas admitted. "Other than try to find another unicorn and who knows where else we'll find one."

"*If* the Comtesse d'whatever her name was is right," Bundersnoot said.

"She's right," Waif said, suddenly. Both Silas and Bundersnoot looked at Waif in confusion and they smiled back. "Something feels right about these woods. Like during the day they seemed ordinary but at night..." Waif paused, looking up at the trees in the moonlight. "I don't know, there just feels something magical about them." Bundersnoot looked at Silas and he could only shrug, equally perplexed as the cat.

"Let's hope you're right, then," Bundersnoot said, curling up into a furry ball. Waif cuddled up around Bundersnoot and soon both of them were deep asleep. Silas tried falling asleep but found his heart was racing far too fast for him to do more than shut his eyes. No matter how he tossed and turned he just couldn't seem to get comfortable, his mind going over how little time he had left. Finally Silas gave up and quietly left the campsite, confident that nothing would endanger his sleeping ward and cat.

Unsure of what he wanted to do Silas walked towards the imperials' camp, drawn by the music and the laughter. It seemed despite the bad blood among family members, the nobility were determined to have a good time. He noticed movement at the edge of the camp, two figures slipping between the guards on patrol and running towards the woods.

SOMEWHERE NEAR TEVIOCH

Curious, Silas walked towards them, cloaking himself in darkness with a minor illusion.

They were young, barely more than sixteen if Silas had to guess. Based on their clothing Silas guessed they were probably servants in the noble retinue, a couple of youths slipping away for a clandestine rendezvous. Silas could hear them giggle as they ran through the open pasture and stumbled into the edge of the forest. As he got closer he could see they hadn't gone terribly far at all into the woods before they had stopped to kiss passionately, locked in an embrace. The two lovers were heedless to the world around them, the girl already working the boy's shirt free from his britches, revealing his wiry body underneath.

Silas would have tsked in disgust, perhaps play a prank on the two before heading back to camp. He never had an interest in pleasures of the flesh and found it a tremendous waste of time. But as the boy took his linen shirt over his head, Silas got a glimpse of his neck and was suddenly consumed by a hunger. His stomach cramped, feeling like a hollow cavity that could never be filled. He could feel his heart racing as he was overwhelmed by the need to consume. He needed…he needed blood. Yes. BLOOD.

"Did you hear something?" the girl asked, pausing as she was undoing the laces of her bodice. She looked around in confusion, trying to find the source of her unease.

"Probably just a small forest animal," the boy said, leaning in to kiss her neck, his hands helping her to remove her clothing. As a result neither of them saw Silas drop his cloak of darkness and strike at the boy with a spell. A small bolt of white light shot from Silas's hand and struck squarely into the boy's back. With no more than a grunt the boy fell over, stunned but for now still alive.

The girl saw Silas and screamed in terror. Without a moment's hesitation she ran, fleeing into the woods. Something in Silas thrilled at the prospect of a chase and before he knew what he was doing, Silas was running after her. The girl was young, nimble, and extremely motivated but even with the light of the moon she could not see as well as Silas could in the dark. Inevitably she stumbled over the detritus of the forest floor and lost ground as Silas gained. Silas had never felt his muscles thrum with energy like this before. Running was sheer pleasure, intensified by the knowledge that his prey was at the end of this chase.

The girl tripped again and before she could get back up Silas was there, looming over her with terrible finality. She trembled, overwhelmed with fear and unable to force her limbs to carry her even an inch further away. Silas smiled, his hunt had come to an end and now, now he would get to feed. His teeth ached in anticipation and he could already taste the warm, coppery blood flooding into his mouth. He reached out and grabbed the girl's hair in his hand, pulling her head back and exposing her neck. She whimpered and tried to flee but one look into Silas's eyes and all resistance fled her body. Silas knelt down and ran his tongue over his teeth, feeling his canines extend. He leaned forward and was about to bite into the girl's supple neck, ready to embrace the hunger inside of him.

And then the world was filled with blinding white light. Silas fell to the ground, all of his senses overwhelmed. He lost his grip on his staff and the girl and he flailed around desperately, trying to get some sort of orientation. Silas felt rather than saw the unicorn approach, the silhouette of a horned quadruped appearing in his mind with the blinding white light behind

SOMEWHERE NEAR TEVIOCH

it. He felt its magical presence, no her definitely a her, brush against him and then voice entered his mind.

You have traveled far, wizard, and I see the darkness inside you. You are close to being consumed by that evil hunger. I can keep it at bay for a time, but no more.

"Please," Silas said, gasping for air as he felt like every part of him was on fire. "I think I have a cure but I need your help. Please, honored one." He tried but there were no more words that he could dredge forth to make his case. He felt the unicorn delve into his very soul, every detail of his life and every secret laid bare. Surely this was what it felt like to be in the presence of divinity.

Yes. This might work. However I cannot aid you as greater dangers threaten my wood. I must first deal with the Enslaver's children. Silas could feel the contempt behind those last two words. *But we do not have much time. Were I not here, you would have succumbed to the curse tonight.*

"I...I can try to help," Silas managed to croak the words. "There might be a way I can scare the Comtesse and her party off."

Very well. When the Enslaver's kin are gone, come to the center of the Lightwood. I shall meet you there. And as suddenly as her presence had arrived it was gone. Silas blinked as his eyes slowly adjusted, realizing he was just a few yards from his own camp. Of the girl or her lover there was no sign. Wearily Silas managed to walk the short distance back to his bedroll and fell into an uninterrupted slumber.

* * *

"Do we have a plan?" Bundersnoot asked as they watched the

Amastican nobility begin their hunt. The beaters were already advancing into the woods, thrashing the undergrowth with great oak clubs and startling any and all animals from cover. Squirrels, rabbits, deer, and birds of a dozen descriptions all fled from the advancing party. The Comtesse and her retinue were riding sedately, interested in only one specific type of game today.

"Rough outline of one," Silas said, watching the forest animals fleeing from the hunting party. He wanted a specific animal, surely the Lightwood had at least *one* fox. If he could just find….there! Slipping through the underbrush and almost blending in was the rust-red coat of a fox. Patiently Silas prepared a spell, collecting strands of energy that would strengthen and enlarge the creature. He would probably only get one chance at this so his timing needed to be perfect.

The fox jumped onto a fallen log and stopped to look back, gauging the distance between itself and its pursuers. As quick as he could, Silas launched his spell, a bundle of green magical energy flying across the forest floor. And in that moment the fox leapt off of the log and disappeared into the forest.

It turned out that the fox was a crafty creature, well used to large groups of humans attempting to catch it and paid the hunting party no more mind than a mountain does the weather. The fox, in fact, was running from an extremely irate goose who was pursuing maternal protection of her children with single-minded devotion. Several things proceeded to happen in rapid succession.

Silas swore and attempted to dispel his enchantment, which failed as even an expert wizard has trouble unraveling a spell on the fly. The goose, determined to exact vengeance from the fox, jumped onto the fallen log that the fox had vacated. The spell, continuing on its trajectory, then collided with the goose and proceeded to do what Silas had told it to do resulting in a goose somewhere around ten feet in height.

"**HONK.**" said the goose.

"Oh no," said Silas.

"Oh my," said Waif.

"Oh fu-" Bundersnoot's comment was cut off by what happened next. The hunting party, shocked at the sudden appearance of a Goose of Extremely Unusual Size, panicked and proceeded to charge at the goose with their lances leveled. Geese are ill-tempered creatures at even the best of times and this particular goose was having an especially stressful day. The goose decided that *someone* was going to pay for it and attacked the closest knight. His horse whinnied in fear as the goose grabbed the knight in its beak, there was an audible crack as the knight's bronze breastplate shattered. The knight screamed in pain as blood and viscera dripped down the goose's snowy white feathers.

The goose threw the knight into a tree at bone-breaking speed and honked triumphantly. Undeterred, three more knights charged at the goose and managed to wound it with their lances. They gave a hurrah as the goose's blood gushed forth but this turned to confusion as the bleeding stopped and the goose's wounds knit themselves back together before their eyes.

"You mixed a healing spell with an enlargement spell?" Bundersnoot asked.

"I was aiming for the fox."

"Is this bad?" Waif asked. "This looks bad." The goose hissed and charged at the closest knight, bowling his horse over and pinning him to the ground beneath it. The goose then turned on the other knights who were making a valiant effort to escape.

"That goose is going to be nigh invincible for the next...let's call it six hours or so," Silas said.

"And you were going to do this to a fox?" Waif asked.

"Foxes at least are cunning. Geese are just wicked." By this time the goose had run the hundred feet or so through the pasture and was now trampling the collection of tents the nobles had pitched the day before. Servants were fleeing in terror as Comtesse d'Jumentpâturage and her armed retainers tried to kill the rampaging goose, all thoughts of the unicorn they were trying to hunt gone. So far it seemed the goose was getting the better of this conflict. "Come on, this should be enough of a distraction. Let's go meet this unicorn."

* * *

Their journey through Lightwood was incredibly swift, especially compared to their stumbling and frustrated efforts of yesterday. The forest seemed to open a path for them to follow and they quickly made their way into the depths of the wood. Mighty oaks, maples, and elms blotted out the sun with their branches, creating a sort of green underworld of the forest. Occasionally animals would stop to look at the party, Silas leading the mare as Waif and Bundersnoot followed, and then return to their business after concluding these humans posed no threat. Birds sang overhead and somewhere in the distance was the sound of running water.

Abruptly they entered a forest glade, blinking in the sudden sunlight. Waif stood gobsmacked, overwhelmed by every color imaginable represented by the plethora of wildflowers.

Common flowers such as poppies, trilliums, and violets grew intermingled among rarer, magical flowers such as the black fahtaire and octarine grass. The mare whickered nervously and pulled against her bridle.

"Silas, I don't like any of this." Silas looked down at Bundersnoot and so much of his fur was on end that the cat looked like a ball of orange dandelion fluff. "There's an absurdly high amount of magic here. This isn't an ordinary glade, this is somebody's garden."

"Do unicorns keep gardens?" Waif asked.

"Don't know, I've never met one," Silas said. "You can stay here if you want, but this is where I need to be." He tugged on the horse's bridle and forced her to follow him into the glade, carefully avoiding treading on any of the more outright magical plants. Without hesitation, Waif followed, carefully keeping in Silas's footsteps. Bundersnoot remained on the edge where the forest ended, eyeing the all too perfect glade with outright suspicion. As his humans got further away, Bundersnoot ended up muttering to himself as he followed, "The things I go through to keep my humans alive. Still, it's easier than training new humans."

As Silas walked into the glade he was overcome with two distinct and almost contradictory feelings. The first was the sense of overwhelming magical power. He wanted to grind his back teeth into dust, that was how much they itched from the raw magic that flowed around him. Almost any work of great magic probably could be accomplished in this place thanks to the wellspring of magical energy that hummed around them. No wonder Bundersnoot, more deeply attuned to magic's ebbs and flows than even Silas, distrusted this place with a passion.

Despite this danger, Silas was not afraid because of the

second, far more powerful feeling. Silas was enveloped in a deep sense of peace. He felt as safe in this glade as he had tucked in his bed on a cold winter's night when he was a boy, buried under a thick wool blanket. Nothing bad could possibly happen to him here, he was past all of the bad things and inside a place that was somewhere…else. In other conditions, Silas could see how he might be concerned by this development, but he was just so tired that this was a welcome rather than a warning.

It had been a journey of hundreds – no, thousands – of miles and many sleepless nights as he was plagued by what could be. Searching for answers, gathering resources, and never knowing for certain whether it would work or not. Silas felt every one of his many decades and was just exhausted from the effort. If he lay down in this glade and died, fated to sleep for eternity, Silas would welcome such an end. His only regret would be those he left behind.

Guiltily, he looked back at Waif, who was entranced by the beauty of this place. There was so much potential in that child, they could be a truly powerful wizard one day with the right training. *Gods*, he thought, *if any of you are listening and inclined to spare my life, don't do it for my sake; I know I've lived long enough. Just give me enough time to help Waif until they can stand on their own.*

"So what do we do now?" Waif asked, finally joining Silas at a moss-covered stone, worn smooth by age.

"Wait, I suppose. The unicorn didn't give me any more instructions than that."

"Probably waiting around to make a dramatic entrance," Bundersnoot grumped, making his way through a clump of white carnations. "Always a fan of the dramatic entrances, unicorns."

"It is part of our nature," a voice said, and the unicorn was *there*. Bundersnoot yowled in surprise and jumped in the air, his claws extended. Landing without injury, the cat turned to find the unicorn standing behind him. There had been no warning; it just suddenly *was* in a place where, a moment before, it most definitely *wasn't*. It was difficult to judge the unicorn's emotions but it seemed to radiate an aura of smug amusement at Bundersnoot's reaction. "Besides, you handled my problem of the Comtesse d'Jumentpâturage's hunting party in a rather dramatic fashion yourselves."

There was no mistaking this unicorn with the creatures which the imperial cavalry rode. Those had been magnificent beasts, refined to perfection by magic but still with a substantial realness to them. This unicorn, a true unicorn, had an undeniable aura of otherworldliness imbued in its being. Its horn was a delicate whorl with the luminescence of pearl, revealing a rainbow sheen in the spring sunlight. A shaggy, white mane spread around the unicorn's neck, much like a lion's, but far shorter. Its legs were delicate and looked too thin to support even the dainty weight of the unicorn, but they ended in cloven hooves which looked as black and sharp as obsidian. Anyone who tried to harm this unicorn would not need to fear its horn, but the hooves were another matter.

Silas bowed to the unicorn. "We are honored by your presence, noble one. Am I correct in concluding I have satisfied your requirements for your aid?"

"You have," the unicorn said, stepping forward and trampling not a single wildflower beneath its hooves. "Your quest is at an end, master Silas. Please show me your wound." It felt more like a command than a request and Silas did not hesitate in rolling up his left sleeve, revealing the long black streak that ran up his arm towards his torso. The unicorn dipped their head down and examined the wound with one eye. The unicorn gave a snort and looked at Silas. "A good thing I found you when I did. Any longer delay and you would have been beyond even my power."

"Then you can cure me?" Silas felt a flare of hope in his chest, a wellspring of emotion he had not dared to let himself feel with even the most minor of successes.

"I am but a conduit for the larger spell," the unicorn said gravely. "I have aided two others with this very affliction many centuries ago but it worked only once. Have you the poison?"

Silas nodded and walked back to the horse and opened one saddlebag, pulling out a pair of thick leather gloves which he donned. He then opened another saddlebag and withdrew the tightly bound leather bundle with the manticore's stinger inside. "Let me see," the unicorn instructed and Silas carefully unwrapped the stinger, keeping his protected hands well away from the deadly object. The unicorn's head dipped towards the stinger and it sniffed tentatively. It let out another snort. "Still potent. Very good. Lie down on that rock." The unicorn nodded towards the moss-covered rock and Silas went to obey, cautious with his burden.

The rock itself was surprisingly comfortable thanks to the thick moss forming a soft mattress. The stone was contoured in such a way that Silas felt cradled, a sensation that further increased his sense of safety and serenity. "Waif, Bundersnoot, I want you to take up positions on either side of Silas," the unicorn commanded. Bundersnoot jumped onto the rock and walked around Silas until he was standing to Silas's right. Waif did not climb onto the rock but stood within arm's reach on

Silas's left. The unicorn took a position directly in front of Silas and took a deep breath as if to steady itself.

"As this may not work, I would advise if there was anything anybody wanted to say, now would be the time." The unicorn pawed at the ground awkwardly and didn't make direct eye contact, trying to give at least a sense it wasn't intruding on a deeply personal moment.

Silas turned to Waif. "Waif, I know we've dragged you from one end of Amastica to the other and beyond. This hasn't been an easy year for any of us. But you've learned so much and I think you'll make a fantastic wizard one day. I just hope I'll be there to teach you."

Waif reached out and touched Silas's arm, keeping well away from the manticore's stinger. "You and Bundersnoot took me in when you had no obligation to do so. You've made me feel so welcome in your lives, I can't imagine living anywhere else now." Waif rubbed their arm across their eyes to wipe away the tears threatening to burst forth.

"Silas, you could have had the decency to make sure I was fed before you died," Bundersnoot said and both Silas and Waif laughed at the cat's joke.

"Bundersnoot, we fed you this morning," Silas said, headbutting the cat playfully.

"I know, but there's always time for another meal." The cat bopped Silas's head gently with one paw. "If this doesn't work, I'll take care of Waif. You can count on that."

Silas turned to look at the unicorn. "All right, I guess I'm as ready as I'll ever be." He took the manticore stinger in his gloved hands and pointed it towards his chest.

"I would advise against stabbing yourself there," the unicorn said.

Silas raised a quizzical eyebrow. "Whyever not? We're trying to kill me, aren't we?"

"Yes, but the poison will work regardless of where it enters your body. If you stab yourself there it's more likely you'll damage an organ that I can't repair. It will work just as well if you stab yourself in your arm or your leg. It may hurt less as well."

"Oh," Silas said. "Well that makes tons of sense. Thank you." Silas pulled up his robe to reveal his left leg and readjusted his grip on the stinger. He steadied himself with a deep breath and before he could have second thoughts, he plunged the stinger into his thigh.

Instantly, Silas was overwhelmed with excruciating pain. It felt like molten bronze had been poured into his leg and was rapidly spreading through his body from the wound. The entire world around him disappeared behind a haze of pain that made him insensate to everything else. Silas gasped as the fire climbed up his leg, into his torso, slowly enough to make the anticipation almost as bad as the pain itself. His breath started coming in short, labored gasps and his heart raced as the fire settled in his belly. He started to feel like he was being squeezed by a tremendous weight. Just when he thought the pain had reached its apex, somehow, it managed to get worse. At some point Silas stopped feeling anything at all.

Overwhelmed by the agony, he blacked out. And then there was…nothing.

* * *

When someone dies or is on the brink of death, and is brought back, there is usually a moment where the person takes a deep breath as they rise, as if launched by springs, from a prone to sitting position. This is all very dramatic and serves to let observers know that the person in question is very much Not Dead. But in actuality, this rarely happens. Usually because whatever made the person die in the first place took a lot out of them physically and they simply don't have the energy to pop up like a jack-in-the-box. Silas's return to the world of the living was no different in this regard.

* * *

The first thing Silas noticed, once the pain was gone, was how very comfortable he was. Most people wouldn't think a moss-covered rock would make a very good bed but Silas was more comfortable than he had been in a very, very long time. The second thing he noticed were the voices talking over him.

"How much longer do we wait? It's been at least ten minutes." Silas's brain sparked and he connected the voice with a name: Bundersnoot.

"You may wait as long as you desire." This voice was warm and pure as silver; Silas couldn't quite place the name. "But I sense that the magic is done."

"Hang on, I think I can hear him breathing again." Suddenly, a tremendous weight was on Silas's chest and he let out a groan of pain.

"Did you hear that?" a third voice now. That's right, Waif. That voice belonged to Waif. "He's alive! Bundersnoot, get off of him."

"That could have just been air escaping from the lungs," Bundersnoot said. "There's no guarantee that he's alive."

Slowly, Silas managed to lift his eyelids. How did it feel like such an effort? Every day he woke up and never thought about opening his eyes. At first all he could see were fuzzy shapes and the suggestion of color. He blinked, control of his eyelids coming easier this time with practice, and after a few seconds everything came into focus. "Bundersnoot," he wheezed, the words coming out no louder than a whisper. "If you don't get off of my chest there will be no chicken for a month."

"Empress and little fishes, he's alive!"

"Bundersnoot, he said get off."

"He just died and came back to life, he's clearly not thinking straight."

Waif pushed Bundersnoot off Silas, who sighed in relief at the removal of several pounds of indignant cat. With limbs that felt like lead Silas slowly managed to push himself into a sitting position. "Thank you, Waif, that's much better."

"Dad! I thought we'd lost you!" Waif tackled Silas and he almost fell back onto the mossy rock from this new attack. Somehow, Silas managed to lift one arm and give Waif an ineffective pat on the back. Waif eventually leaned back, their cheeks streaked with tears of relief. "I was so scared."

"Well, it would be irresponsible of me to leave you alone with just Bundersnoot. Although I have to ask, when did this 'dad' business start?"

"Sometime around Coursuperieur," Bundersnoot said, looking rather smug that he had known something Silas hadn't. Waif merely blushed with embarrassment.

"Sorry, it started as a joke between Bundersnoot and me and then…kind of stopped being a joke," they said, looking away nervously. "I can stop if you want me to."

"Waif, I have spent over fifty years adventuring across Amastica, and a good portion of those years with Bundersnoot.

SOMEWHERE NEAR TEVIOCH

I did not expect to become a parent at this time of my life, or quite frankly ever." Waif looked crestfallen but Silas continued. "However, if you're willing to claim a cranky old wizard as your parent, who am I to argue? *Of course* you can call me that, Waif." Waif smiled and hugged Silas again, granted more gently than last time.

"Ah, I see, the critical component," the unicorn said. Everyone looked up at them in confusion. "The manticore venom, my own power – they helped but they were not what broke the curse."

"Love," Silas said. He wasn't sure why he was so surprised, remembering two young women he had helped. One had been turned into a werewolf, the other had her daughter stolen by the Fae. Silas had helped both of them but in the end the most vital component had been love. Love of a father and brother had broken the curse of the werewolf; love of a mother had helped her identify her child from a Changeling. And for him…

"Yes," the unicorn said, interrupting Silas's chain of thought. "The love of two people who cared about you deeply was what broke the vampiric curse. You are indeed most fortunate, wizard Silas. However, I must now take my leave of you."

"Already?" Silas wasn't sure he'd be able to stand, much less walk, and it was such a long way back to their campsite.

"You all may spend the night here in my glade; no danger shall befall you. My people have spent many centuries fighting She Who Reigns as well as Her descendants. There are many tasks and never enough of us to complete them, so I am called elsewhere. Wizard Silas." The unicorn dipped their head in respect. "It is unlikely we shall meet again, but I was happy to be of service. Perhaps one day you will do my people as great a favor." And with that the unicorn turned and walked away.

One moment it was still there and then the next it was gone entirely.

"Bah, unicorns," Bundersnoot said, climbing into Silas's lap and settling down into a loaf. "Overly dramatic, from the tips of their pearly horns to the golden hairs of their tails."

"And they can't count," Silas said.

"What makes you say that?" Bundersnoot asked.

"Well, the unicorn said there were two people who loved me enough to break a curse. You'd think even a unicorn could tell the difference between one and two. Unless, Bundersnoot, there was something you'd care to admit?" Bundersnoot said nothing but tried, unconvincingly, to make sounds that he was fast asleep. "Typical cat," Silas said, and gave Bundersnoot's ears a scratch before lying back down onto the rock.

"So what happens next?" Waif asked, joining Silas on the natural bed.

"In the short term, I'm getting some sleep. But tomorrow, we're going to head back home."

* * *

Somewhere at the edge of the forest, a now ordinary-sized goose approached Silas's wagon. It had had an extremely long and tiring day of putting the fear of the Empress into quite a few people and was now extremely hungry. Its attempt to return home to its farm and enjoy a meal of hay and grain had been thwarted by a very scared farmer and her husband shooing the goose away with brooms. No matter how much it had hissed at them, they had been determined to keep the goose from entering the farm and the farmer suspected the goose was now home of some malicious spirit.

Now the goose smelled food and flew the short distance into the bed of the wagon. It poked and prodded at various bundles until a supply of dried peas spilled from a sack, which the goose ate with enthusiasm. It was still an angry goose, but it was now an angry, fed goose which was a considerable improvement. The goose fluffed its feathers and tucked its head under its wing, settling in to sleep. Who knew what tomorrow would bring?

II

Appendix

If my readers will indulge me in my pretensions of being a Fantasy Writer™, I have decided to include an appendix providing more information on a few topics briefly mentioned or touched upon in this book. If you are an individual who finds such material to be so much extra homework, I will not be offended if you decide to skip it. Congratulations! You've reached the end of the book! Go get yourself a nice snack. But if you are a sucker for fantasy lore then by all means, please read on.

- Kalpar

The Empress Allie

Foreword to *The Dawn of History: Collected Essays on The Empress Allie* (Citadel University Press, 2123 Benlin Calendar), written by Professor Addler Pfeiffer, Citadel University.

There are few figures in history or mythology that cast as long a shadow as Empress Allie the Great, often referred to simply as "the Empress" for there is no need to refer to another. Indeed, her existence has permeated into every aspect of life in Amastica and many lands beyond. She is worshiped as a god by an estimated one third of the world's population, some who fervently seek her return. The Amastican calendar, at time of writing currently in its three thousandth one hundredth and twenty-second year, officially began with the Empress's coronation in Tevioch. History began with the Empress, for she rendered all that came before her irrelevant.

Like so many figures of such magnitude, the Empress blurs the lines between history and mythology. Ironically, as one delves into documents closer to the time of the Empress, what is fact and what is fiction becomes much harder to parse. This appears to have been part of a deliberate campaign by the Empress, shrouding her origins with contradictory stories and exaggerating (or more often understating) her powers as a wizard. At best, the honest historian can create only a rough sketch of what is generally accepted as true about Empress Allie, and leave the artistic details to those less chained to facts.

What we know for certain, through recovered documents and archaeological digs, is that what is now Amastica was inhabited by city-states which utilized both bronze tools and magic as early as seven thousand years ago. Approximately thirty-three hundred years ago, many of these cities were utterly destroyed and later deliberately rebuilt around the same time. We know this due to the presence of the Schliemann Layer, a distinct layer of detritus in the archaeological record discovered by archaeologist Henrietta Schliemann in 1868 (Benlin Calendar). Imperial-style circle cities were constructed on top of the Schliemann Layer, connecting it with Amastican activity. This correlates with the time period when Allie, not yet Empress, is believed to have emerged from the Land of the Fae with her armies of elven warriors.

After her coronation as Empress, Allie consolidated and expanded her empire for three centuries before, if records are to be believed, she returned with the majority of her elven warhost into the Land of the Fae. Supreme executive authority was invested in her eldest surviving daughter, the Empress-Regent Grâce I, the first of a long line of empress-regents. After the Amastican year 313, Allie is definitively put in the past tense. There is hope that she will one day return, but as far as the imperial government is concerned, she is no longer here.

Some of my colleagues, most notably Dr. Tagus of Wotansburg University, believe that Empress Allie is in fact a composite character made of multiple historical figures to give the Amastican Empire a mythic origin. Although compelling, Dr.

Tagus's theory simply does not match our available evidence. The deification of the Empress did not begin until the mid-500s of the Amastican calendar, well after she disappeared from living memory. Furthermore, what documents we *do* have from the first through third centuries of the Empire definitively, without *any* deviation, refer to a singular Empress Allie. Surely, if there had been multiple empresses during this period we would have found evidence for at least one of them.

History is seldom a story of Great People but rather the story of small, incremental changes over time. Look no further than our own nation of Benlin: Legend says the five and twenty clans were first united under Thundrykk Ironhammer, first High Krynn. While Ironhammer's influence was important, the clans had been forming into a more cohesive political entity under outside pressures for decades. The appointing of a High Krynn merely finished what had already started. The only definitive exception to the rule appears to be the Empress, and I doubt she'd have it any other way.

The War of Faeborn Succession

Excerpt from *Encyclopædia Amastica*, digital edition, retrieved 15 Third Month 2124 (Benlin Calendar)

The death of Empress-Regent Grâce IX, last woman of the Faeborn Line, ended over twelve centuries of rule by direct matrilineal descendants of Empress Allie the Great. Initially it appeared the entire Amastican Empire, the greatest power the world had known, would descend into the chaos of civil war. The sons and spare daughters of the Faeborn house had been numerous over the centuries and had married into the many noble families of their empire, cementing alliances between locals and the imperial center. They had been so numerous that most baronnes and even a few of the landed chevaliers could in some way claim descent from the Empress. Arguably anyone had a claim to the throne.

By law and tradition, however, only a wizard could claim the throne, and she would need both a strong matrilineal claim and sufficient support from the Imperial College of Wizards to do so. Realistically, there were only two claimants with sufficient power and influence to make a proper bid for the throne: Rachelle Silverbark and Lier Cascade. The Silverbark and Cascade families had long been bitter rivals within the

Imperial College and both families were well-placed to stake their claims.

Rachelle Silverbark, Marquise d'Ganorne and Supreme Vicereyne Beyond the Braelors, appeared the obvious choice to many contemporaries. The Silverbarks had long been considered politically reliable by both empress-regents and the College, and accordingly had been granted wide latitude in administrating the outlying territories beyond the Braelor Mountains. Although sparsely populated, this coastal region offered immense resources and controlled the only means of contact with the colonies in New Amastica across the sea. The Silverbarks also commanded over twenty thousand of the best, most experienced soldiers within the entire empire. If Rachelle had left for Tevioch immediately upon word of Grâce IX's death it is very possible she could have become empress-regent herself, but for whatever reason, she remained in her provincial capital of Fons-voc.

The Cascades, by contrast, had never enjoyed the popularity of the Silverbarks. Long distrusted by the Faeborns, the Cascades had been kept close to court in Tevioch and controlled relatively few holdings. Lier Cascade, scion of the Cascade family and Duchesse d'Portereine, listed only ten armed retainers in 1475 and her assets consisted of a villa in Tevioch and the Duchy of Portereine, which gave her an income of a mere 1,000 livre per annum. However, her proximity to power meant Lier had spent many years learning the machinery of the Imperial College and was a deft hand at parliamentary manipulation. Although intensely disliked, members of the College ignored Lier at their peril and the same would prove true for Rachelle.

Lier entered the power vacuum left by the empress-regent's

death and within six months had managed to cajole, coerce, or bribe enough members of the College for her to be made empress-regent by acclamation. When word reached Rachelle that her rival had been crowned Lier III, she is said to have smashed her crystal ball with a warhammer in rage at the news. Spurred by this insult, Rachelle declared herself the true empress-regent and ordered all her armies to meet at the city of Elade-voc in preparation for a march on Tevioch to depose the usurper Lier.

If Rachelle had struck even a month before Lier's coronation, she and the Silverbarks most likely would have secured the imperium. Unfortunately, once Lier had been acclaimed, the immense resources of the imperial heartlands were at her disposal. The majority of the imperial army, some quarter of a million soldiers, were at her command and the income of the Faeborn holdings, estimated between 100-125,000 livre per annum, provided a much-needed influx of ready cash. Finally, simple geography was in Lier's favor. By placing an imperial army at the town of Coursuperieur, Lier effectively bottled Rachelle's forces in the only pass across the Braelors. With winter approaching, Rachelle had no choice but to strike a prepared enemy.

The Battle of Coursuperieur, the first battle of the War of Faeborn Succession, was a rousing victory for Rachelle and her army. The imperial defenses consisted of a simple pentagon fort and a series of earthworks rapidly constructed by the imperial army. The majority of the imperial troops had seen only garrison service and were unprepared for the hard-bitten veterans of Rachelle's own army. Despite these advantages, Rachelle lost nearly two thousand men in the assault on Coursuperieur, casualties she could ill afford, and the majority of the imperial army retreated in good order with their baggage train. Running short on food and other supplies, Rachelle had to force her army forward once again.

The Siege of Orvion would prove to be another Pyrrhic victory for Rachelle. She handily defeated the imperial field army outside the city in a pincer movement, robbing Orvion of defenders at a critical moment. As she invested the city many smaller ladies of the outlying lands joined her ranks, swelling her host to some thirty thousand, which put further stress on her already shaky logistics. Unable due to politics and logistics to maintain a siege, Rachelle ordered a rapid assault on the city. Once again, her corps of veteran soldiers carried the day, but once again the victory would come with steep casualties. How the fire started is still a matter of debate, but it quickly spread through Orvion and consumed the city. All efforts to stop the blaze failed and it continued for three days until a rainstorm managed to finally quench the flames. The foodstuffs Rachelle had hoped to feed her army with were gone, and all that remained was a slurry of ashes.

Faced with no better options, Rachelle split her army into four columns and ordered them to march in the general direction of Tevioch, living off the land as they went. This simplified her logistical problems but created new issues of command and control. If Rachelle had been blessed with competent and charismatic subordinates, her plan may have worked, but once again fate conspired against her. Many of the small ladies and their retinues deserted, sapping the strength of her divided columns and leaving them dangerously exposed. Lier's generals, informed by deserters of this situation, decided to defeat Rachelle's army in detail.

Mélissa Archambault's column, already winnowed to three

thousand soldiers due to desertions, was surrounded by an imperial army ten times its size. It was utterly destroyed. Rachelle only learned of Archambault's defeat when her own outriders came across the mass grave of the battle. Rachelle hastily attempted to re-concentrate her forces but another column was encircled and destroyed before they received their orders. Without enough soldiers to strike at Tevioch, Rachelle immediately began retreat towards Coursuperieur and the resources of her own dominion. But imperial forces beat her to the pass first and, lacking the strength to retake Coursuperieur by strength of arms, Rachelle and her troops melted into the countryside.

The next eleven years would turn into a grueling campaign as Rachelle's forces attacked targets of opportunity and avoided direct confrontation with the imperial military. Many attempts were made to break through the Braelors and reinforce Rachelle, but none succeeded and her troops underwent slow attrition over the years. Her steadfast refusal to be lured into open battle once again ensured the conflict endured. It was only the sudden death of Lier III and succession by her daughter, Grâce X, in 1487 that allowed the conflict to end. Grâce X offered a general amnesty to Rachelle Silverbark, her kindred, and all her soldiers on condition that they should voluntarily take exile to New Amastica. Exhausted by over a decade of war, Rachelle agreed.

Thus the War of Faeborn Succession, which opened so aggressively at the waters of Coursuperieur, was quietly ended before the walls of Tevioch. The Cascades had secured the throne, but in so doing had cut the empire off from its trans-Braelor territories for a decade. The imperial hand would only rest lightly on these lands until the arrival of the Rusting Death.

A Short History of Elade-voc

Taken from *Elade-voc: Crossroads of Commerce*, informational brochure published by the Elade-voc Chamber of Commerce, 3120 (Amastican Calendar)

Elade-voc, which translates from Old Amastican to "Crossroads City," was founded by Empress-Regent Grâce V in the year 813 as a fortress at the joining of the Ganorne and Fallingbank Rivers. This fortress controlled navigation of both rivers and secured imperial control of the east end of the pass carved through the Braelor Mountains by the Ganorne River. Archaeological evidence suggests that the site of Elade-voc may have been a popular trading point even before the imperial garrison, but the added security provided by the garrison made it even more attractive to merchants. By 829, a sufficiently large population had grown up around around the fortress that Grace V granted the community the traditional city charter of rights and established local government.

The presence of the river trade, as well as the construction of the Imperial Highways starting in 874, meant that Elade-voc continued to prosper, and by 1010 the city was granted the right of crenelation. The city walls constructed during that era are preserved to this day and remain a beautiful tourist attraction in the inner city. However, the War of Faeborn Succession would bring about dramatic changes for Elade-voc. Stripped of its imperial garrison and left largely to their own devices, the Council of Elders of the city declared Elade-voc to be independent of the Empire and took over all aspects of city governance, including the maintenance of the garrison and collection and administration of trade tariffs. The Empire, beset by civil war, was unable to stop and Elade-voc continued to flourish as a center of commerce.

Elade-voc would remain independent until they voluntarily, and with no coercion whatsoever, joined the Coastal Republic in 1805 as a charter member. In the modern era, Elade-voc continues to foster a business-friendly environment that has been the city's life blood for millennia-

Brochure continues with description of Elade-voc's tax-friendly government and loose regulatory policy. I deemed it irrelevant. – K

Map of Eastern Amastica

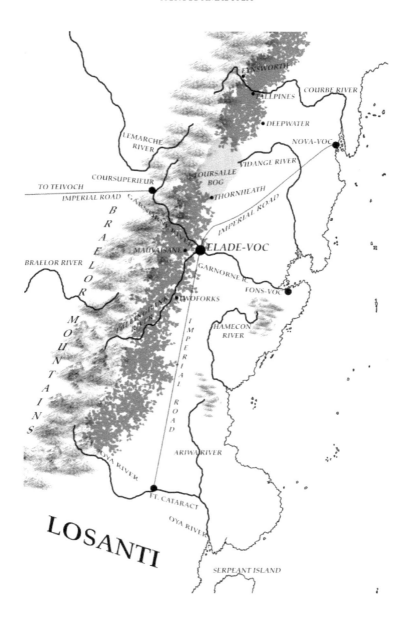

About the Author

Writer, historian, ferroequinologist, numismatist, polymath. These and other fancy words can all be applied to Kalpar with varying degrees of accuracy. Kalpar is the pen-name of B.A. Klapper, a born and raised Cincinnatian who lives there to this day with their loving and supportive spouse. Kalpar is a non-binary individual who uses they/them pronouns.

You can connect with me on:

https://www.thekalpar.com

https://www.facebook.com/profile.php?id=61552351350395

Subscribe to my newsletter:

https://buttondown.email/Kalpar

Also by Kalpar

Silas & Bundersnoot

A cozy novella about a wizard and his cat as they tackle the magical intrigues that find their way to their doorstep. Days will be saved, villains will be foiled, and perhaps, most shockingly of all, Bundersnoot will miss a meal. But that's just a potential danger of the job.

Milton Keynes UK
Ingram Content Group UK Ltd.
UKHW040940141024
449705UK00005B/200